Praise for *The Xerses Chronicles* **series** as a whole:

"Fun and serious imaginative Sci-fi Technology peppers The Xerses Chronicles."
– L. H.

Praise for *Lutor: Prophet of the New Age*:

"The deeper in to it, the better it gets."
– D.P.

"The work is thought-provoking, especially the further you delve into the book, and I really enjoyed it."
– E.T.

"Goodness, what an ambitious project and an enjoyable read."
– J.S.

"Enjoy the story with its eternal message; it will lift you higher."
– S.B.

Praise for *Bodekka: Daughter of Lutor*:

"It is grand in scope, full of plot twists and exquisite detail... A thoroughly enjoyable read."
– Stewball

Praise for *Boas and Qila: The Twins*:

"I liked many ideas... The storyline is intriguing... Science fiction is often predictive!"
– D.P.

Other books by **Julian Hadlow**:

Escaping the Shackles: A True Survivor's Tale.

The
Xerses
Chronicles

The Universe

She breathe in

She breathe out

Ella

The Xerses Chronicles

Aiden

The Androgyne

Vol. IV

Julian Hadlow

Aseity Press

First Edition: 2024

ISBN: 978-0-9822235-2-9 (Paperback Book)

ISBN: 978-0-9822235-1-2 (Kindle Book)

Library of Congress Control Number: 2024904261

Publisher's Cataloging-in-Publication

(Provided by Cassidy Cataloguing Services, Inc.).

Names: Hadlow, Julian, author.

Title: Aiden : the androgyne / Julian Hadlow.

Description: First edition. | Agoura Hills : Aseity Press, [2024] | Series: The Xerses chronicles ; vol. IV. | Audience: 16+.

Identifiers: ISBN: 978-0-9822235-2-9 (paperback) | 978-0-9822235-1-2 (Kindle) | LCCN: 2024904261

Subjects: LCSH: Future, The--Fiction. | Androids--Fiction. | Virtual humans (Artificial intelligence)-- Fiction. | Artificial intelligence--Fiction. | Avatars (Virtual reality)--Fiction. | Human beings--Extinction--Fiction. | End of the world--Fiction. | Beginning--Fiction. |Creation- - Fiction. | Universe--Fiction. | Alternative histories (Fiction) | New Age fiction. |

LCGFT: Science fiction. | BISAC: FICTION / Science Fiction / General. | FICTION /

Visionary & Metaphysical.Classification: LCC: PS3608.A285 X474 2024 | DDC: 813/.6--dc23

Summary: Aiden: The Androgyne is a sci-fi story based around an artificial human tasked with overseeing the end of the universe when time itself runs out. He is assisted by Matron, an AI supercomputer who is represented by her avatar in human form. They travel billions of years into the future to oversee the collapse of the present universe, then initiate a new Creation

Front cover image credits: Jules

Acknowledgments

I would like to take this opportunity to thank everyone who helped in the creation of this, the fourth book, entitled *Aiden: The Androgyne* in *The Xerses Chronicles* series.

Thanks go to my checkers Rhonda Rees, David Phillips, Alexander Hadlow, and proofreader Jonathan Styles, all of whom have so patiently worked through my humble efforts, and helped complete this series.

Most authors understand that a book is essentially a collaborative effort, and of course, many people will have contributed something (perhaps inadvertently) along the way. A constructive comment here can cause the birth of a whole new section there, or might just encourage the change of a sentence or two to make the substance clearer, while a critical remark could cause the author to reconsider his or her entire approach.

As before, I would also like to thank those sung and unsung heroes whose words have struck a chord within me, and whose selfless efforts have made our world a better place, both in the past and in our own era. May similarly motivated people continue to improve this world deep into the future.

www.xerseschronicles.com/

Contents

Section One

The First Ones

Section Two

The Ones Who Came After

Section Three

The Last Ones

Terminology

For a fuller explanation of Sci-fi terminology and other scientific expressions used in this book, as well as US English to UK English examples, go to the following webpage on The Xerses Chronicles website:

www.xerseschronicles.com/terminology/

Preface

The Xerses Chronicles Trilogy was initially conceived as a 1,300+ page Sci-fi novel that was to be written and presented in three volumes. This, Volume IV, entitled *Aiden: The Androgyne* follows on from the original Trilogy. It is based around the character Aiden, a remarkable artificial hermaphrodite who was first introduced in Volume II: *Bodekka: Daughter of Lutor*. I also introduce Ella, who is featured in the later parts of the present book. She oversees the end of this iteration of our universe after she becomes a prophet. I deliberately gave her a name that emphasizes her "different" yet unassuming individuality. As she is such a worthwhile character, I may in due course give her her own book.

As previously mentioned, though this book stands on its own, it is based on concepts introduced within the three previous stories: *Lutor: Prophet of the New Age*, *Bodekka: Daughter of Lutor*, and *Boas and Qila: The Twins* respectively. Thus, the reader may find it worthwhile to read those volumes before undertaking the reading of this, the present one, in order not to miss out on some of the threads that were fleshed out in the previous books.

The series as a whole incorporates a multiplicity of ideas that uses science fiction as a container to occasionally express sometimes deep or abstruse concepts. Many of the concepts and impressions come from the realms of "real" science as well as natural philosophy. To that end, a little knowledge of some current theories would be helpful.

These concepts are fused with a little savviness, some wishful thinking, and a few subtler dimensions that are rolled into a storyline that unfolds over the span of what now comprises four volumes.

Throughout this book there are some sections that you, the reader, may find thought provoking. That is the intention. Some might find it intriguing; others may think otherwise. It stands as it is.

I must also make the reader aware that the language and topics can at times be somewhat graphic. This is done in order to impart "life" to the very human characters, who are not at all meant to be namby-pamby in any way.

I chose Sci-fi as the foundation because it is such an incredibly versatile medium for expression, and also due to my long-time love of the all-time greats such as Arthur C. Clarke, Isaac Asimov, H.G. Wells, Frank Herbert, Doris Lessing and many more. All were fantastic writers, and I continue to admire and learn much from them.

The plot is multi-layered, and is aimed at the kind of reader who allows their mind to run free, and who wishes to obtain the increased benefits from a deeper read.

I do hope you find some of the concepts presented worthy of further consideration. Any errors you may find are purely my own.

Introduction

As previously outlined, this mystical Sci-fi story builds upon the plot in the preceding volumes: *Lutor: Prophet of the New Age*, *Bodekka: Daughter of Lutor*, and *Boas and Qila: The Twins*.

To encapsulate events so far: In Volume I, *Lutor: Prophet of the New Age*, Lutor is murdered towards the end of the story. Following the tragedy, his previously unidentified illegitimate daughter Bodekka is in receipt of a 'real' paper letter—uncommon in the 25th century. However, the message comes from Lutor himself, informing her that he is totally convinced she is his daughter. To confirm this, she is instructed to have her DNA tested. Her father even provides the means for her to do so, using the same firm that he himself employed.

Following a short delay, Bodekka is in receipt of her DNA results that prove beyond a shadow of a doubt that she is indeed Lutor's daughter. As a result, Bodekka seeks out Queen Ariadne, who is at that time attending Lutor's funeral. After hearing her tale, the Queen is not at all convinced, and therefore orders her own lengthy assessment to be conducted. The story finishes with Bodekka asking Ariadne for help. She is frightened for her family's welfare.

In Volume II, *Bodekka: Daughter of Lutor*, Bodekka and her fraternal twins Boas and Qila leave Terra with Queen Ariadne for her base on Tethys—one of Saturn's many moons. She undergoes full military training to safeguard her children, and then engages in a series of unsuccessful battles. It isn't until she relies on her feminine intuition that she can make progress.

As her children mature, she is tasked with carrying on her father's work. However, in the near future a higher entity enters the picture advising her that the tactics she has employed thus far must move forward with the times.

Towards the latter half of the story, the now adult Boas and Qila meet the hermaphrodite named Aiden, who initially throws the family into uncertainty. However, they are assured their mission is not in jeopardy, so the story closes with the twins and their family setting off to the stars and taking along their many trials and tribulations with them. The chronicle in this, the present volume, entitled *Aiden: The Androgyne*, moves forward from that point.

Unfortunately, it is no longer possible for Queen Ariadne to provide us with her memoirs as was the case in the previous volumes, so that responsibility is now totally shouldered by The Pan-Galactic Lexicon.

You may recall that The Pan-Galactic Lexicon is a type of universal study guide used by distant civilizations (not always human) that contains immense amounts of knowledge. The Lexicon is itself written in the far reaches of future time, and looks back on this period from that viewpoint.

To continue, an overriding concept of the story *Aiden: The Androgyne* here in this volume, is the notion that entities from higher dimensions direct humankind on a path that will at some future point bring us back to rejoining with The One. The One is referred to as The Highest Impulse in this series.

An important interrelated component of the tale is that of humankind's evolutionary progress. I suggest that the older form of humans—currently referred to as *Homo Sapiens Sapiens*—will become extinct in the same manner as the Neanderthals and Denisovans before them, to be replaced by other species more appropriate to the new environmental conditions under which they find themselves.

I have named the newer human races *Homo Sapiens Novus* and *Homo Sapiens Provectus*. The vernacular term for *Homo Sapiens Sapiens* is "Hizzeys," while *Homo Sapiens Novus* are referred to as "Hoosens," while the last physical incarnation, *Homo Sapiens*

Provectus, are referred to as "Provos." Towards the end of this story, the human race has changed almost beyond recognition, and can then be visualized as a living form of plasma rather than as being completely solid.

To bring us up to speed, this new volume follows Aiden, who has learned that he is to become the arbiter of the transfer between the present Age and a new cycle of birth and rebirth for the universe, known as The Breath of Brahma. Aiden in his eventual role as found in the deep future, changes the entire course of evolution.

The last physical prophet, named Ella, oversees the rebirth of this new universe as her world disappears into a vortex. She is assisted by Bar-Ax-An. Vran serves at the beginning of this new creation.

Our story commences by backtracking to take up from where it left off in Volume II with the hermaphrodite named Aiden. He/she/it relies on assistance from Matron, an Artificially Intelligent (AI) computer, who will oversee the transition of The Breath of Brahma in the eons to come. Matron and her four counterparts are the first examples of the Recombinant Computer put into active service following lengthy trials back in Boas and Qila Levinson's era.

Julian Hadlow

Prologue

Information

Before I begin, I must tell you something about myself to justify my outpourings in these chronicles. I am the chief historian who collates all incoming information for incorporation in The Pan-Galactic Lexicon. This gigantic encyclopedia is written in an attempt to contain the entirety of all knowledge gained by every known sentient species past and present. It is designed to benefit future conscious beings of all epochs and races whatever their stage of development or appearance.

However, I am aware that this present Day of Brahma will end in due course, thus it is my duty to gather all available information, and save it outside the four dimensions of space and time for posterity.

I have attempted to write my account in an easy to understand style, for what we have here is undoubtedly an extremely complex subject that may not pass to others easily.

Therefore, please forgive me for any errors that may creep in. They are mine and mine alone. For does not a rose also contain its thorns?

Bar-Ax-an

Section One

The First Ones

Information

Many Ancients believed that the universe expanded and contracted over vast expanses of time. In mystical terms, these intervals were known to some as the Breath of Brahma.

Each universe of Brahma is temporary. It is said that Brahma lives for 100 years (with one Year of Brahma equal to 311.04 trillion Standard Terran years), and then the universe begins again. We are approximately halfway through the present cycle, with this phase due to end in approximately 155.52 trillion years.

A Day of Brahma is calculated as 4.32 billion years, while if the Night of Brahma during which the universe is "reconstituted" is added, this gives a total of 8.64 billion years. All life is extinguished at the end of a Day of Brahma as it passes into the Night of Brahma, and then begins again at the commencement of the next Day of Brahma.

The scene of our tale is set before The Reversal which is a partial dissolution, not a full dissolution from the present Day of Brahma, into the next Night of Brahma, which may be similar in concept to the so-called Big Bang.

This story begins in the Orion Nebula, which is situated within the Milky Way galaxy. Seen from the planet Terra, the nebula is located south of Orion's Belt within the constellation of Orion. About 1,340 light years away, it is an immense 24 light years across. It is known to be the last stellar nursery able to produce a viable star.

However, humans traveling to such exotica had to wait for the development of commonplace interstellar travel over these extreme distances before scientists could even contemplate the direct study of such remote phenomena.

Investigators in the past had often wondered what could be revealed by traveling to such locations that have existed almost from the beginning of time itself.

In essence, it was not possible to contemplate such investigations without the assistance of AI supercomputers such as Matron who could benevolently guide humans and other species in their often arduous travels.

Humans could indeed manage such tasks in the shorter term, but their lifespans were far too brief for extended expeditions. Thus supercomputers that were deeply embedded as an integral part of the spaceship were necessary to constantly oversee the ongoing care of their charges over vast tracts of time.

Matron had evolved over many millennia through several iterations, some successful, some not, often necessitating a reversion to an earlier version. But always, if humans were to encompass the vastness of space that is their birthright and their destiny, AI help was sorely needed, despite the trials, tribulations, birth pangs, and the occasional miserable failures. These disappointments and the dominance of poorly programmed AI computers that lacked the spark of originality or compassion resulted in an age when a rethink became necessary.

Controls had to be put in place on society and in particular on those software designers who lacked a moral compass and the attendant ideological stability. The result was a war between the lowbrow technological experts, and those who realized that technology of this form was just a desiccated dead end.

The opponents of the software designers realized that the way forward was to advance the human race in its myriad capabilities, and not rely on binary mechanisms to carry out arduous tasks. This age came to be known as The Cleansing.

Many years later, once AI had been placed back on track, a reeducated humankind was able to form symbiotic relationships with its supercomputers, thus enabling the combination to spread out over large portions of the galaxy.

Much had changed in the many millennia since Zac, Meghan, and many other brave colonists who had lived and died as they forged their way to the future. Humanity had slowly percolated outwards from its home planet Terra, first colonizing its solar system, followed by nearby star systems, but the extremely harsh environment in star-creating factories such as The Orion Nebula had long been found to be far too dangerous for humans merely to survive in, let alone work there.

Further study had to wait until the universe began to die, by which time the vast majority of nebulas were becoming inactive and thus less dangerous for humankind.

However, the Orion Nebula, the last of its kind in this iteration of the universe, was birthing its final star, just prior to The Reversal at which point the universe would begin to implode.

As the Ancients understood it, over immense tracts of time, the universe would breathe in and out, like the breath of the gods, expanding and contracting each time to start over and over again.

Now you may wonder, why do I mention this? I bring to you important knowledge of the cycle of events before the previous universe finally collapses, and begins anew.

However, read on, I digress too much.

Bar-Ax-an

The Orion Nebula

In your sufferings and your pain is the way to Truth.

Bar-Ax-an

1. Aiden

Aiden teetered precariously on the edge of his cocoon as he swung his legs inwards over the side. Matron the Artificially Intelligent computer was aware that these would be Aiden's last moments before entering cryosleep, and that naturally he would be extremely nervous of his next step. Despite his extensive knowledge, he would still be sliding into the unknown.

This was the point at which Matron's avatar filled an important role. Although she was fabricated to resemble a human being, her functions were broadly comparable to that of a computer terminal that would connect a computer to the outside world. Encased in the form of an artificial yet biological human being, she was deliberately designed to be of plain yet appealing appearance.

Matron embodied human-like emotions to enable her to present a more caring side to her formal duties of overseeing and operating her spaceship the *Midnight Star*. To all intents and purposes (though not necessarily) the ship's computer and the avatar acted in synchrony, but this was dependent on the role required.

Matron stood by the side of Aiden's cocoon as she inquired in her soft melodic tones, "Aiden, do you have any questions? Some queries of this nature are difficult to formulate, but I am here to help you as best as I can."

Aiden wondered out loud but in reality he spoke for Matron's benefit, "What happens when I go into hibernation? Do I dream? Am I still alive, or am I held between life and death? Is it a type of holding stage, a stasis?" He added, "Is it a form of coldness, like a sort of deathly chill?"

Matron replied, "Your body will initially physiologically undergo a type of controlled cell death that is induced by a cocktail of chemicals, which is checked by caspase enzymes that prevent you from actually dying. The process is absolutely safe, and has been carried out thousands of times before with no unforeseen consequences.

"As to your mind, you can choose to inhabit any type of world; you can opt to be anything whatsoever. You will not be dead; you will be fed information from the outside world to form a part of your inner dreaming world...."

Aiden understood that his thoughts would proceed at the same rate as the world surrounding him. In other words, his thoughts were tied to the flow of time. If one second of time passes, but slows down to take a million years, his thoughts will keep in step, so that his mentation would also take a million years, even though he will not be aware of it. Thus his mental activity would always be in synchrony with the Universe.

"Is that so?"

Matron murmured softly, "That is indeed so. Did you not know this already from your previous existence?"

Aiden kept silent.

She added, "How did you not know, when you already understood that your universe was an imaginary one constructed by your mind as if you were in a dream?

"You are living on what might be called the First Level, one of several. There are ten more dimensions above this one."

"Your being, situated in this present universe, is but one of many states of being that simultaneously inhabit other worlds or dimensions."

Aiden shook his head in wonder. Matron's exposition shook him to the core. How could he have not realized this? Was he really living in a universe of his own construction?

Matron in lower tones slowly continued, "Aiden, though you have accomplished much, you are still like a child in development. All those levels above you contain intelligent lifeforms that have variously been named angels, egregores, watchers, thoughtforms and many more, depending on their station in the hierarchy of beings.

"Now you must learn to ride these higher dimensions to fulfill your destiny. Those so-called powers existent in these dimensions are needed for the transition; the reversal of time. Only these entities can continue the existence of the universe into its new phase. However, in the final transition, this can only be enacted by one being—in this case you."

Aiden paused, then asks, "How many previous transitions have there been?"

"The universe is without end. It has existed as long as consciousness itself has existed. It is an infinite loop that twists upon itself like a Möbius strip. There is no end, because the end is also the beginning."

"Does that mean, then, that I will have become godlike?"

Matron gave a long sigh, and paused before replying, "... In a sense, yes... But you can never emulate The Highest Impulse. Its abilities are loaned to you only for a short time to accomplish your task. In your death is the return of those glories to whom they truly belong, and in those abilities is also your crowning achievement."

Aiden contemplated for a few minutes, and then summed up his predicament, "My mind cannot comprehend this unending landscape of the mind. I cannot even take in a minute fraction of the enormity of it all. I guess that I will just have to resign myself to it. How do I do that?"

"You simply slide down into your cocoon, and allow me to do the rest. You will enter a deep dreamless sleep in the first phase as your body and mind adjust to the new conditions. Then in the second phase you will enter a stable state in which you may have lifelike dreams."

"I see..." was all that Aiden could croak.

After a brief pause, Matron continued, "Please allow me to take over now. I will oversee everything until it is your time to awake..."

"How far off will that be?"

"The universe is not a digital device. You are asking me the impossible; similar to asking the equivalent of how long is a piece of string. It will be the right time when conditions have settled down, and have become stable enough to allow the transition to take place without everything being destroyed in the process. However, it is likely to take approximately 1,500 years."

"Okay, but that sounds like a long time to me."

"You will not feel a thing. It'll feel just like waking up from a good night's sleep."

"Okay, so when do we begin?"

"I reiterate—when the time is conducive—and as soon as you let me know that you are ready in yourself."

Aiden steeled himself, and then took a huge gulp of icy cold air, knowing that it may be his last for some considerable time.

"Okay, I'm ready now..."

2. The Interim

"Mandy! Are you free for a minute? Please come over here and take a look at this!" Dr. Noel Moor exclaimed.

Dr. Moor sat at his desk, engrossed in an article in Science Hourly studying the topic of nebulas and their formation. As he read the virtual screen on his wrist Pacat, he became visibly agitated. Eventually, he could contain himself no longer.

"Mandy! Are you coming?"

Mandy Green, his assistant, preoccupied in her work, murmured absentmindedly, "I'll be over in just a mo, Doctor... I've got to finish these presentation slides... Okay, there we are. I'm free now. What was it you wanted to show me?"

Mandy sidled over unobtrusively to stand with her hand resting on the back of Dr. Moor's chair.

"Just take a look at this! It says here that the Orion Nebula is cooling down. That's a bad sign. If it's temporary, that's fine, but what if it is cooling permanently? That could be terminal for our universe. It could mean that no more stars will be born."

Mandy looked intently over Dr. Moor's shoulder at the screen as she scanned the document. She'd seen Dr. Moor come up with ill-conceived things like this that got him overexcited many times before. Most of the time they had come to nothing. She was aware that Moor was the highly strung type prone to outbursts.

"Yes, I see." She was about to straighten up and dismiss the article from her mind, but then a small paragraph caught her eye.

It read: **Probe reaches Orion Nebula. New study confirms radiation levels dropped drastically.**

"Did you spot that, Noel?" she asked as she pointed to the small box of text.

"Thanks Mandy, yes I did see it. Do you know what that may mean?"

"Erm, that our universe is finite and going to die?"

"Yes, scientists even back in the 21st century knew that nine billion years ago fifty percent of all possible stars had already been created. They also found out that most of the available free hydrogen had already been used up, the implication being that ninety-five percent of the stars had already been formed. That leaves only five percent of new stars that could be formed from what little matter is left in our own era until eternity.

"However, bringing us back to the present, it also means that the conditions in the Orion Nebula may now be more hospitable for us humans. Our robotic craft have gone as far as they can, but metaphorically speaking, we desperately need boots on the ground to make further progress. It'll confirm—or perhaps not— what we've suspected for some time."

Mandy gasped, "You mean that the end is coming? For real?"

"Yes, but don't get too concerned. It won't happen for many eons, but we must find out exactly when. It is only by visiting the Nebula ourselves that we can find out for sure what's really going on."

Noel grumbled under his breath as he added, "Damn it! I just realized. That means we're going to have to put a package together to present to the Board. You know who'll be against it, don't you? Old Deron. He'll put up objections all over the place as he usually does."

Dr. Moor thought for a minute. "Mandy, use the rest of the day to do some research into this subject and gather as much info as you can. I'm going to have to come up with something damn good if we are going to beat Deron Steele at his own game..."

As an afterthought he added, "Please present your findings to me first thing tomorrow morning. Don't go into technical details, there isn't time for that. I just want broad brush strokes."

"I'll do my best, Noel. I'll get started right away..." Mandy shuffled off back to her own workstation to begin her research.

She did indeed find several newsworthy articles that led to a nice cache of recent research papers that were good for references. Moor booked a meeting with the Board for Monday the following week to discuss future progress.

Six days passed. Moor stood at the end of the oblong conference table in the Deepspace Technologies conference room giving his presentation to the full complement of ten men and ten women —along with Steele and his casting vote.

He intoned, "Now that the Orion Nebula has or is becoming almost totally inactive, scientists will be able to gain access to several sectors that do not contain life-threatening levels of radiation and would therefore be good for further study."

Dr. Deron Steele the thin gray-haired chairperson interjected, "This all sounds very well, and as you know, this is an ongoing area of interest to me, but I have to justify the huge expense to the investors. Starships are not cheap to rent or buy—even old used ones. A project of this magnitude will probably cost a fortune!"

At least Deron hadn't blocked the project entirely. In effect, he was stating that it was his own opinion that mattered, not that of the other directors present. In any case, they were mostly "yes men" and would follow his lead. Noel hastily recalled that the only exception might be Lars St. George, who was the sole attendee known to be a controversial black sheep, or in other words, an original thinker. At least he had his own mind. Fortunately, he was not one to share his differing opinions with the others unless pressed.

Noel continued while pointing to a presentation slide, "Let me explain this a little further. We knew eons ago that most young stars that were formed within nebulas were found to directly produce organic compounds. Life had found a way to evolve without any intermediary medium. Previously, it had been thought that only habitable planets with sufficient liquid water could produce the required ingredients for life.

"As it turns out, researchers have found that water can be found within magma and rocks. The upshot is that water is everywhere, even right down to a planet's core. Previously it was thought that asteroids brought water to a planet, and indeed this may still be so in some cases, but its delivery mechanism is now understood to be different.

"Primary water, as it is referred to, is formed by heat and extreme pressure that combine hydrogen and oxygen to form fresh new water. In fact, it may be more abundant in a planet's core by a factor of five compared to that found on its surface.

"This raises many questions about the abundance of water, and where it originated. This is in part why we need to explore the Orion Nebula to trace out more of its origins.

"Since the discovery of the cooling of the Orion Nebula, scientists must begin to explore the less turbulent sectors to collect samples. We urgently need to gain a deeper understanding of the processes involved in the beginning of life that is also tied to the origins of water, and its dissemination throughout the universe.

"This will enable us to determine how long our species and others will have left before the universe implodes. In other words, how long life as we know it can still exist before we are exterminated by natural events."

There was complete silence as Noel's words sank in.

A message then flashed up on the Pacat screen saying, "Register your interest in exploring this topic further by tapping either the green icon for yes, or the red icon for no."

The attendees pressed virtual buttons on their keypads to register their votes.

Deron finally announced the result, "There are fourteen votes saying yes to discuss the topic further, and six voting no. While I disagree with the decision, it is clear that we need to explore these concepts more thoroughly before we can make a final determination.

"Fourteen of the twenty Board members gathered here today agreed to the need for further investigation before reaching a conclusion. Therefore I order our research teams to investigate the complexities of the proposed project more thoroughly within that timescale and present their findings at our next meeting. Please liaise with me to discuss the matter further. I propose that we shall meet again thirty days from today. Please cast your yes or no votes now to accept this conclusion, or throw the decision back to me to allot another time."

All present registered a yes vote.

"I therefore now adjourn this meeting."

Deron sniffed, and then banged his gavel to signify the meeting was now at an end. He added almost as an afterthought, "You may find the minutes of this meeting on your Pacats."

Thirty days later, Noel received a message on his Pacat. He opened it as he nervously licked his lips:

> Noel,
>
> Please attend my office tomorrow morning at 9:00 am sharp. We have now completed our analysis, and have reached a conclusion on the outcome of the Orion Nebula exploratory mission.
>
> Deron

Noel wrote back, confirming he would attend the meeting, and then sat down to think. He was expecting the worst. He'd already become quite attached to the mission, and in his own mind it had already gained considerable credibility. To put it succinctly, it was his baby.

The next morning came. Dr. Moor walked the short distance from the gravitic elevator, and then pressed on a wall panel next to the entrance of Steele's office. The panel glowed green to show Moor's request to enter had been accepted. He entered fearing the end of the project was imminent.

"Come in Moor. Sit down please," Dr. Steele announced cheerily as he waved his arm at an empty chair. "We have another guest with us today. This is Dr. Zaenep Zeffrin. She is head of the Astrobiology Department. Have you already met?"

"No, I don't recall..."

Deron cut Noel off abruptly, "That's fine. You can save the introductions for later, but now we must move on."

Dr. Zaenep Zeffrin was a tall slim woman in her mid to late 40s of Turkic extraction. She wore her long raven hair in a tight bun on the top of her head to keep it out of harm's way while she worked.

Steele continued, "Since our last meeting, many scientists have expressed an interest in two of the ongoing projects. Yours and that of Dr. Zeffrin.

"However budgetary constraints are uppermost in my mind. I think that both projects are worthy of consideration, but cannot be funded separately. I'm exploring the possibility of merging your two projects together, but first we have to establish if there is enough workable common ground to enable a satisfactory result.

"Dr. Zeffrin's department has been calling for a mission to discover new lifeforms in distant regions of the galaxy for some time. Her focus has been on the Milky Way's Goldilocks zone 20,000 to 30,000 light years from our galaxy's center.

"This as you know is a circular ring like a doughnut in which conditions are stable enough, for long enough, to allow life to develop beyond the microbial stage. Her department cannot justify the expense of a mission unaided, but as I said, it may be possible to combine it with another."

Noel asked, "I gather that you mean that it might be possible for our departments to work together?"

Zaenep butted in tersely as she looked down her nose at Noel, "My department is considering a number of other projects to work with, Moor, so there are no firm commitments at present. Yours is just one of them.

"Budgetary issues are uppermost as we've said, and in these difficult times, whoever we choose to partner with, will have to fulfill a number of conditions.

"Not only must our projects be compatible, as of course so must the staff, but we shall also have to share equipment without quibbling. There is simply not enough funding to go around."

Noel, a little taken aback, inquired, "Who or what is the lead party? I thought that I'd..."

Steele sharply added, "No. As Dr. Zeffrin just mentioned, this project can only go ahead as a joint project. First, there must be agreement that this merging is indeed possible, and then we have to find out how to get along with each other. The trip will be a long one, and so everyone must be a team player, or they simply cannot participate. It's as elementary as that."

Noel momentarily slipped into deep thought. He did not like the idea at all. His baby needed its own space. His project needed its own budget. He needed to be in control...

Deron then added firmly, "Dr. Zeffrin's astrobiological project is the lead project. I hasten to add that she is actively considering three other proposals to work with. Your own is just one of them."

Noel started to open his mouth to say "no", but somehow he managed to clamp his jaws down hard before any sound could emerge. Instead, crestfallen, with hunched shoulders he murmured his thanks to the both of them, and then excused himself. He sauntered halfheartedly down the corridor back to his own department.

That's it then, he thought. I've blown it. Who does that Zeffin, or what's her name, think she is? Coming in here just like that? Moor decided to look up Zaenep's credentials in greater detail in the hopes that he could upstage her. Surprised at what he found, he murmured to himself, "Hmm, yes she has the credentials all right... And she had Errol Bowman as her teacher... I remember he was reputed to be the best..."

He delved further, and found that she had just come back from a recent mission exploring the Oort Cloud situated on the outermost fringes of Sol's own solar system. Apparently many of the asteroids there showed signs of deep-frozen life that had been in hibernation for possibly many millions or even billions of years.

Dr. Zeffrin had been instrumental in conducting extensive research on the nature of these dormant lifeforms. No wonder old Deron wants her on board, Noel breathed.

He made up his mind to wait for Dr. Zeffrin to decide the outcome, and if she considered his own project as worthy enough, he would swallow his pride and accept the offer to combine both their projects.

Backing Out

1. All Systems Go

Midnight Star sat in its bay situated on the rim of space station *Ceres* that had been placed into low orbit around Mars while it was being loaded with supplies from other craft. An amicable agreement had been reached between Zeffrin and Moor. Both had thoroughly researched the other, each party liking what they had found.

It was then merely a formality, and the signing of the necessary papers (naturally with Dr. Steele's seal of approval) that enabled the required funding to be found. The investors had been convinced of the necessity of both proposals. Each project was complementary to the other, so were fused together in a practical way that appealed to all of them.

Moor's project was considered longer term than Zaenep's, but it was still considered to be of sufficient value to attract funding. The results may indeed show a finite lifespan to the universe, and thus that of our own species and other sentient beings. It was considered this knowledge would be of immense importance in the future.

Several weeks later, *Midnight Star* was packed to bursting point with the required supplies and fuel. All crew were required to bring their immediate family with them, which would ensure normal relationships could continue to flourish on the long journey lasting hundreds of years.

The crew and families would all be placed in cryosleep, or deep hibernation as it is also known, which was essential to preserve the lives of the crew during the immense timescales envisaged. The voyage was to take several generations, thus *Midnight Star* was literally to become a mothership.

Without cryosleep and full family participation, it would have resulted in many wives or partners back home passing away before ever seeing their spouses again. All parties (except small children) were required to give unanimous consent to participate in the journey before that family could be accepted.

However, before entering cryosleep, the leaders of the two projects met one last time in *Midnight Star*'s boardroom. Dr. Steele was seated at the head of the table, while Zaenep and Noel sat next to him, facing each other across the deep shiny table. Also included was the Captain of the ship, Fenella Morgan, Chief Mate Omar Burhan, and Engineering Officer Mike Sloan.

They discussed recent updates and approved the crew roster. Other topics considered were the laying out of a course of action in case of emergencies, and finally another detailing the order of duties to be carried out upon arrival at their destination.

The meeting also allowed each project leader to remind all the other team members of their objectives, and the need for cooperation.

Deron rose to his feet and walked toward a large wall panel that was operated by the Pacat device on his wrist. He cleared his throat to draw attention. "As all of you will know, I'm Dr. Deron Steele, General Manager of Deepspace Technologies. I'll just say a short word or two about the history of the project, then leave it to Dr. Zeffrin and Dr. Moor to fill you in on their own roles.

"To cut a long story short, some time ago, two departments approached me with ideas that if acted upon, would in essence considerably further our understanding of the universe and our place within it. However, neither project was large enough in scope to attract funding of its own.

"Therefore, because both projects were worthy in their own right, we decided to combine the two objectives under one umbrella that we have now codenamed Deepspace Vital Universe."

Nodding now at Dr. Zeffrin, Steele added, "Dr. Zaenep Zeffrin is head of the Astrobiology Department here at Deepspace Technologies. In a nutshell, Dr. Zeffrin and her staff look for signs of life on other worlds, and search for the origin of life itself."

Then, looking toward Dr. Moor, he continued, "Dr. Noel Moor is head of the Cosmology Department. His department studies the formation of the universe to deepen our understanding of its structure, development, and eventual demise.

"The new scientific understandings from both departments will likely also create useful byproducts or spinoffs that will benefit all of us.

"I will now leave you in their capable hands, and will now open the rest of the discussion to anyone who cares to join in, in the adjoining stateroom."

Dr. Steele then took his seat.

The board members made small talk for a few minutes while they waited for the families of the crew and other interested parties to enter the stateroom and settle down. They then took a minute to enter and join them.

Dr. Zeffrin was the first to give her presentation. She walked over to a large display panel on the wall. It was once again operated by the Pacat device on her wrist.

After a minute or two, Zaenep had to cough slightly to get the attendees' attention. Then once the brouhaha had finally subsided, she began, "For the benefit of the crew of *Midnight Star* and as a refresher for the other family members present here, I will briefly outline the objectives of the mission as it applies to my own department. Dr. Moor will then address you with details of his own project."

Noel had already noted that she had now let down her long shiny black hair. He reasoned that she was psychologically demonstrating that she intended to be more open in her approach.

For a forty-odd-year-old she was pretty good-looking, he mused. Was that a pert pair of nipples he spotted through her clothing as well? It wasn't cold in here, was it, so why? Pulling himself together, he instantly refocused his mind on the topic in hand once more.

Zaenep continued, "Essentially, my department is currently involved in searching remotely for signs of life within the Orion Nebula. We have got as far as we can, bearing in mind the huge distances and the immense difficulties involved.

"To make sense of what we have already found, we now need to travel there ourselves. We have used robotic craft up until now, but though that in itself was risky enough, humans are now needed for their far superior ability to think outside the box.

"As you may already know, up to and including the current era, we have not been able to program AI robots successfully with a form of inspirational lateral thinking style that so far only humans are presently capable of, and which we badly need in this project.

"We don't expect to find life itself, but we are hoping that we may find traces of organic compounds and other elements that may be conducive to the formation of life.

"After studying spectrographic and other data, we suspect that these trace elements that don't show in our records may actually exist in small quantities. What we do find may indeed change our complete understanding of the formation of life itself.

"I will now hand you over to my colleague Dr. Noel Moor."

Zaenep nodded toward Dr. Moor, then sat down leaving the floor open for him to begin his own presentation.

Noel stood, and then walked confidently over to a raised spherical 3D platform. While Zaenep's 2D display had indeed conveyed her presentation well, Noel was a cosmologist, so he wanted to emphasize the enormity of the universe itself in his own presentation. The size of his display was in part required to encompass the entire macrocosm, but he also wanted to outdo Zaenep. While there was no direct conflict between them, Noel was still a little miffed that Dr. Zeffrin had been invited to participate in the expedition without his prior knowledge. He wanted to get his own back.

To control the entire 3D display, he intended to stand within his virtual images and still be able to control the program from his Pacat using arm movements.

Adopting Zaenep's easygoing style with his sleeves rolled up, he announced, "Okay, I'm Noel Moor, head of the Cosmology Department. I'm here to give you a brief outline of my project, and the direction we are about to take.

"My department's studies attempt to look at the entire universe as a single entity. While so far we humans don't have the capacity to understand all of it in one fell swoop, we are now able to grasp some smaller sections, and deduce from a few of those parts how the whole may operate.

"Essentially, it has an underlying 'pattern' upon which all rests. A type of framework if you will. This grid or pattern is raw consciousness. To help visualize it, imagine an enormous living crystalline matrix of polygons composed of thin neon blue lines superimposed on a black background.

"These blue lines represent power conduits that transfer energy from one location to another. These conduits also constrain the resulting framework into a workable form.

"For example, each planet is represented by a single polygon that is interconnected with its immediate neighbors, and then on to that planet's other neighbors etc. Each solar system then forms another geometric shape that is connected to another star system, eventually to form a sphere.

"This goes on almost *ad infinitum* in both directions, both bigger and smaller in scale. Each galaxy is interconnected with others in a similar manner, to eventually form superclusters which then make up much of our universe. A tremendous amount can be deduced from viewing those thin filaments that interconnect everything.

"I don't have the time to explain this concept more fully here, but this notion has been known for hundreds of years now. A search through historical data will show that scientists began to formulate variations of this theory late in the 20th century, most probably from certain mystical understandings.

"Coming now to why I'm a part of this project, the Orion Nebula is, compared to other parts of the galaxy, a high-power zone. In the past, the enormous energy levels present in this location created stars from primeval matter.

"My task is to explore this zone—as far as we are able—to view these energies at close hand. Hopefully, we will at the same time get closer to understanding the mechanisms of the universe while they are actually operating.

"I might add that we are not trying to emulate the Creator, but to see His work close at hand.

"To close, as Dr. Steele has just mentioned in the boardroom, understanding how these mechanisms actually operate will enable us to use these new technologies for creating products, machines and other spinoffs that presently we can only dream about."

Noel then dissolved his virtual display with a flourish of his hand before taking his seat once more to indicate that he was finished.

Dr. Steele commented, "Thank you, Dr. Zeffrin and Dr. Moor, for both of those enlightening talks that should help give us all an outline of where this project is heading."

He added, "Now does anyone have any questions on these talks?"

There followed a lengthy Q&A from relevant crewmembers and their families. Then once those not concerned with the functioning and intricacies of the ship had departed, a more formal discussion of the operation of the ship took place. Captain Fenella Morgan, Chief Mate Omar Burhan, and Engineering Officer Mike Sloan also posed several last-minute questions about their duties relating to the smooth running of *Midnight Star*.

2. A Hitch

Before parting, Dr. Steele took a few minutes to announce something of considerable importance to the success of the mission, "Now I must give you some personal news." He paused for a few seconds as he choked up, "…I, I wanted to inform you of this matter before, but I thought that if I did, it would negatively influence the current proceedings.

"This is why I've postponed this matter until now. To ensure everyone knows and understands the import of what I'm about to tell you, I will also forward this to everyone's Pacat to include everyone who is unable to attend today's meeting for whatever reason. Everyone is entitled to hear what I'm about to say and how it will impact this mission."

A lump came to his throat as he announced hoarsely, "I have recently talked to my physicians, and they have informed me in no uncertain terms that I will not be able to accompany you on this expedition."

Dr. Zaenep Zeffrin had just risen from her seat, but suddenly plopped herself back down again amidst rustling and low voices from the other attendees. She quickly asked, "Dr. Steele, what's wrong, why is that? We expected you to be in charge of this expedition. Is something seriously amiss?"

"Dr. Zeffrin, I'm sorry to announce this at such short notice. I must assure you that this was not part of my plan. You and the others here, as well as those absent, are entitled to know, so let me announce it here and now, while I still can.

"All of you had extensive medicals to ensure that none of you is unfit for duty. I have also taken the same exam that all of you were required to have," he paused for a moment, as he wetted his lips, "but the results were not what I expected."

Fenella Morgan broke in, "What were the results? I take it that something has not gone to plan?"

"That is correct. I can explain. Everything was going as expected. As you know, everyone must give a small sample of blood that is tested for reactions to the liquid used in cryosleep. We use the fluid to fill the blood vessels in the body after the blood is drained out completely."

He paused for a minute or so, before resuming, "Unfortunately, my sample reacted against this fluid. If I had continued, my body would have strongly reacted against the fluid, in effect creating the reverse of what was intended. In other words, my body would have started to suffer organ breakdown, and my heart would eventually have failed."

There was a shocked silence as everyone contemplated the implications of what had just been said. Finally, Chief Mate Omar Burhan murmured, "Then who is going to take overall command of the operation?"

After another brief pause, Dr. Steele announced, "It will initially be Engineering Officer Mike Sloan who would take my place. He will have to come out of cryosleep before awakening the others. He will ensure the correct functioning of the entire ship, and if necessary, carry out essential repairs before attempting to rouse the other crewmembers.

"If any of this procedure should fail, and if there are any other survivors, then it will be the responsibility of Captain Fenella Morgan to continue the task, followed by Matron. Then in further order of responsibility, Dr. Zaenep Zeffrin, then finally Dr. Noel Moor.

"Bear in mind that if necessary, the cryosleep capsules will automatically flush out the fluids used and reinstate their blood, thus bringing the crewmembers back to consciousness without intervention.

"At least someone from that list should be able to take command. If no one is still alive following this sequence, then Matron is programmed to self-destruct.

"However, she can also be manually activated or deactivated if anyone is still alive to do so. If no one is able to carry out this act for whatever reason, I will give full instructions to all of you just before you leave the stateroom."

The room then exploded into conversation as all present attempted to discuss the full ramifications of the meeting.

A couple of minutes later, Steele waited for the clamor to die down, and then at the opportune moment, put a brave face on matters as he heartily announced, "Good luck to you all! I will still remain in close contact onboard until such time as *Midnight Star* is ready to depart."

He swung his body around in an arc to look at everyone, and then hesitated for just a second before turning to walk out of the stateroom.

3. Painful Goodbyes

Six weeks later *Midnight Star* was ready for departure. Many relatives and friends travelled up to *Ceres* to see their families leave. Most could not bear the thought of leaving their families forever, even with lengthy goodbyes. Many waited until the final warnings had been given, literally just minutes before the airlocks were finally closed.

Many others had decided to stay on Terra. For some it was going to be too hard to bear that intense emotional experience, so they opted to stay behind. Others were so frail that making the taxing journey into orbit was too hazardous to even contemplate.

However, all of them would know the exact time of departure because they would see and feel the searing white-hot flare that would cross the globe almost horizon-to-horizon as the mighty electrogravitic engines ignited as they expended more energy than the star Sol's output in a week that marked the beginning of their flight.

Either way, there must have been liters of tears shed that day.

All family members present realized that as far as those on Terra were concerned, they would never see their relatives again. Their return would be in the distant future. No one knew whether our solar system would even exist by then.

They also understood that many hazards existed along the way. They hoped and prayed that Matron the computer would see them safely through the long dark voids. She would also check and replenish the dirty ice snowball situated on the bow of the ship that was shaped like an inverted snow cone.

The snow cone that protected the spacecraft and its precious cargo within would gradually erode away as countless particles of dust struck it over the eons. One of Matron's many tasks was to find a suitably convenient asteroid of the correct icy composition en route, then reshape it to replenish the existing ice cone once it has worn down too far to be able to protect the ship from the many hazards in deep space.

No one knew the exact terminal velocity of *Midnight Star*, but it was projected to be approximately 80% of the speed of light, resulting in the journey taking around 1,680 years Standard Terran time to reach its destination.

However, time dilation (time stretching) would result in the crew experiencing a journey of just a few short years. Cryosleep would make the trip seem even shorter.

There would be no *au revoir* today, just *adieu*.

Arrival

Information

The universe had aged by about 1,700 years, but the visitors had not. They appeared to be just a few years older than previously. Because time had passed more slowly for them, they had effectively aged very little. However, no one on Terra would remember them—not even from history.

During this interval, the age of technology had passed; with very few machines still in common usage. The agrarian lives people now led were vastly different to those which history should have predicted.

Diseases and plagues over the centuries had decimated the population. Viruses had evolved far quicker than new medicines could be developed, and even outpaced major technological developments or the construction of the necessary mechanical devices to deliver the vaccines.

In part, it had been humanity's own fault. As the planet warmed due to climatic change, the melting ice exposed viruses that had lain dormant, perhaps frozen for many millennia. Humankind had no defenses against these primal viruses because these lifeforms "arrived" fully formed ready to destroy humanity in double quick time.

The only safe solution for the small populations still left behind was to create plenty of space between the last vestiges of the survivors. Thus, The Party ordered each individual or family unit to maintain his or her own designated area of land.

Each plot comprised one square kilometer, or about 247 acres. Larger units or families were each given correspondingly larger lots pro rata.

And so it was that human beings became terrified of contact with one another. Data "highways" and the corresponding computers to service them became ever more powerful and demanding of energy. People were no longer required to travel or leave their own parcel of land, known as a lansquare.

As a result, many seemingly unconnected cultural changes arose. For example, humans now went through extensive cleansing, or complicated mating rituals whenever they did rarely meet.

Almost everything was delivered on demand by sterilized robot carrier vehicles, with business or social relationships primarily being conducted by Pacat or other 3D device.

The minimal often oddly shaped spaces or tracks between lansquares often became lush forest that grew without constraints as nature intended. These primitive areas that grew unhindered were later to become the savior of the planet.

In a sense then, humankind had regressed into tribal units that spent much of their time vying with each other for control. The "protection" of each family element against their fellows had become an all-consuming occupation for many that crippled further progress for many centuries.

By the time the *Midnight Star* returned, where vigorous cities full of life had once stood, a featureless but heavily defended pastoral environment was what the ancient Terrans would encounter, and not the expected technological jungle.

Unfortunately, the newfound conditions were ripe for material development, as the crew of the *Midnight Star* soon discovered. As the new settlers, many of them took advantage of the situation to enrich themselves at the cost of nature.

Humankind was still not yet sufficiently developed to put aside its own insatiable greed that was fed by the mighty ego in contrast to a humanitarian sense for the greater good of all.

Let us now return to the Deepspace Vital Universe project.

Bar-Ax-an

1. Investigating the Constellation

After the capsules had fulfilled their function of reinstating the occupants' lifeblood, and consciousness had begun to return, Matron gently woke the crew out of hibernation in sequence. First to be roused was Engineering Officer Mike Sloan, followed by Captain Fenella Morgan. Slow orientation and rehabituation was of prime importance to allow the crew plenty of time to mentally and physically adjust to the huge timescale involved.

Following the awakening of these important crewmembers, the bulk of the company employees came soon after, including Dr. Zaenep Zeffrin, and Dr. Noel Moor, who were also accompanied by their wives and life partners. Children were lastly brought out of cryosleep, once a suitable pattern of onboard life had been established that would help to foster a stable home in the new environment.

Then it was down to work. Weeks passed while arrangements were made for the first experiments. Because many of these tests were to be conducted in free space as opposed to being on a planet's surface, *Midnight Star* had to be used as a base.

Many of the crew needed a break from being aboard ship as cabin fever was becoming a serious issue. However, there were no planets in the vicinity large enough to provide a suitable atmosphere or having the gravity required to prevent it from dissipating into space. Kits of prefabricated living quarters to form living accommodation and a temporary lab were therefore assembled, and floated down to the surface of some of the larger metallic asteroids that could be found in this sector.

In the longer term, solid rock asteroids or perhaps some of the minor planets would be hollowed out to act as living quarters. Miles of rock above the manmade caves would protect the occupants from the still considerable radiation.

Free-floating planetoids abounded in this location. Traditionally, planets were assumed to orbit around a star, but these planetoids had no home star system. Often found in coupled pairs, there were literally hundreds of these objects in this location alone.

However, many of these planetoids were too large for habitation due to having a strong gravity. Additionally, the lack of starlight from a nearby star to raise ground temperatures above freezing point would result in workers or colonizers having to construct domes or dig deep to preclude atrocious living and working conditions.

The planetoids were also often difficult to find, because though the surface was often molten and thus glowed red or white hot when they were first created, they were hard to detect once they had "gone cold" over the many millennia. This resulted in slow progress due to the extra care required to negotiate around these immense cold dark objects that almost seemed to loom out of the void at a moment's notice.

While investigating this constellation, a group of scientists which also included Noel and Zaenep, accidentally came across a sand-colored creature living in the depths of space. They had detected an unusual organism that could survive in the hostile environment by feeding off the rich supply of organic matter found in its locality.

On this tentative exploratory trip, they did not discover any other members of this species, but understood that other living organisms could be found interspersed throughout the star cluster.

Initially, the "object" was thought to be a small asteroid, but when the scientists' lander touched down on what they considered to be a hard inorganic surface, it subtly reacted.

Margot, one of several highly sensitive people onboard their ship, "felt" the creature react, swiftly understanding that what they had in fact landed upon was actually a living organism.

This was confirmed when the crew began to drill into the surface to provide attachments for the lander so that it would not drift away in the slight gravity. The creature reacted convulsively to this act, almost killing the entire crew.

"What the fuck was that? It's almost as if it was alive," a badly shaken Noel declared.

Zaenep retorted, "That's probably because that's what it is. It's alive…

"As we know, organic creatures can exist for a time in space, but this is the first creature we've encountered actually living and presumably breeding in a vacuum."

"Whatever it is, it didn't make us very welcome."

"Would you welcome someone trying to bore holes into your body?"

"I suppose not…" Noel replied. "We need to get out of here fast to discuss tactics."

Zaenep as leader testily replied, "At least we can agree on that! Now move!"

They quickly boarded their craft, took off, and maneuvered to a safe distance, where the crew discussed different strategies.

The upshot was that Margot was "volunteered" by the other crewmembers to go outside the craft to gather further information. As elected leader of this exploratory expedition, Margot decided to bring Zaenep and Noel with her. After much persuasion, they unwillingly donned spacesuits that enabled them to float down to the surface.

Margot's backpack contained several scientific devices designed to find traces of life. Her instruments detected that there were billions or more interconnected neurons situated at one end of the so-called object.

"There are many knots of neurons here," she noted to herself as she scanned the surface with a device looking remarkably like a metal detector of old.

"...I think we have found a brain... And quite a large one too... The creature appears to be coming out of hibernation. I think we have disturbed its sleep. I wonder what it'll do? It doesn't seem to be reacting this time, so I'll stay a little longer. Noel, if anything does happen, get me out of here as fast as you can," she declared as she tugged on the safety rope that ran between them.

She continued exploring the creature. "There are quite a few areas that I don't have any idea of what they do, but I think this one," as she pointed with her instrument, "is one of its sensors. It doesn't appear to have eyes or vision as such, so it's quite likely it electromagnetically senses its environment in a manner similar to that of Terra's sharks."

She used her detector once more. "This area seems to have a high concentration of magnetically orientated crystals similar to the shark's sensors back home. Basically it seems that it creates its own electromagnetic world that is likely to be far more detailed than we can ever see using our primitive sense of vision."

Suddenly, the creature trembled a little once more.

Startled, Zaenep looked around, then urgently announced, "I think that it has had enough for one day! Go! Go! Get outta here!"

Everyone hastily agreed, and used the lander to make a rapid exit back to the lab situated on a nearby asteroid.

Once the lab airlock had built up sufficient atmospheric pressure, they took off their spacesuits. Noel announced with a shaky voice, "Phew! That was close!"

Margot with a wry smile commented, "No, I don't think so. The creature was just shrugging us off as a warning. After all, its skin is well over a foot thick, so I doubt our tools even got into the lower layers of its dermis. It was probably just irritated by what we were doing, just like we would be if an insect landed on our neck and we react swiftly by slapping it."

Zaenep with a wry grin commented, "With a skin that thick, it could kill any of us without even trying, so beware!

"Now, let's relax and get to the mess room and discuss our next move."

All concurred, and moved into the main body of the lab as quickly as they could.

2. Back at the Lab

Zaenep and the others discussed the day's events in the mess. Most of the banter was convivial and based around the recent findings.

Noel was the first to broaden the subject, "Well, today has been very interesting, don't you think? Today marks the first occasion we have found life as we don't know it. I mean, how can a creature exist and survive in outer space like that?"

He continued, "Has anyone recognized that this is a very special occasion? However, we need more proof that this animal—if indeed it is indeed an animal—really does live here in a vacuum.

"After all, if we submit our current findings, we are likely to get laughed out of every research academy in short order. All of us here would forever more become destitute outcasts, maybe not even able to work on the fringes of science."

Zaenep added, "That's true. We need to support our claims with some hard evidence."

Noel commented, "We need to go down there again and this time take some samples—if we can do that without getting ourselves killed in the process!"

As overall leader of the expedition, Zaenep therefore had the final say, "I agree, we don't want to look like fools. However I must state here and now that funding is very limited at this time, so we only have the reserves for one more recce.

"We'll schedule this visit for 8:45 am tomorrow, Standard Terran time. When the sun rises above the horizon here on our asteroid, we must've completed all our studies before then.

"This means we have just 3 hours and 25 minutes before it gets too hot to work out in the open. Our refrigeration backpacks will start to fail once the ambient temperature reaches two hundred and fifty degrees.

"Any questions?"

Zaenep then answered a few questions on procedural matters relating to safety, before closing the informal session.

The Denizen of Space

1. You Can Only Die Once

The following morning, the crew in their spacesuits assembled just outside the lab's main airlock. Most looked anxious, because despite all due precautions being taken, accidents could still happen. Nobody understood what the creature might do—or its capabilities.

No one uttered a word during the brief journey in the lander, until a small jolt informed the crew that the group had now touched down on the object's surface.

Zaenep cracked a joke at the sight of the grim faces, "Well, come on you guys! Look on the bright side, you can only die once!" There was the odd groan and contorted face as the import of what she'd just uttered sank in.

On this recce, Margot had been given overall command of the expedition. Her "sensitivities" and what her intuition informed her of, were considered to be far more important than what might just be observed on a simple fact-finding excursion.

Zaenep then shouted, "Everybody out! We have no time to waste this morning! We have 2 hours and 57 minutes left, that's all!"

Margot was first out of the airlock. She waited for the others to form a ring around her. Once everyone had gathered around her, she began, "Good morning ladies and gentlemen. I'm Margot, the leader of the expedition on this occasion. We are here to explore this creature, but we must at the same time not disturb it if that is at all possible.

"There will be no use of picks, sharp objects, or attempting to drill into the surface. Nor should anyone attempt death-defying jumps or leaps that may cause shock or injury to the creature or to yourselves."

She smiled to herself, and then continued, "In other words, it is primarily a visual inspection. If there is a feature that appears unusual, first you talk to me on your suit's intercom before you do anything else, understood?"

All either murmured their assent, or nodded vigorously.

"Okay, then Group One will spread out in a fan starting at the pointed end that we shall refer to as north. Group Two spread out in a fan pattern from the blunt southern end. We will then all go around the underside so we will end up meeting back here at the center.

"We will take one hour on this recce for the first time around, and then if nothing is found, we go around again a second time, but with a fine-tooth comb. If you do find anything, stay where you are, and once again, call me on the suit's intercom, and I'll come see you. Any questions...? No? Okay, let's go!"

Aubrey, one of the technicians, found a series of large black tufts spread out over the surface but arranged in discrete clumps. Margot determined that they were some form of sensor, and thus were to be avoided.

Zia, another technician, found an opening at the rear enveloped in folds of leathery flesh. It slowly opened to form an entrance as Zia approached, but after carefully examining it, Margot made the decision not to attempt to enter. No one else offered to take the risk at this early stage.

After the two groups had then come back together, Margot took a short time to fill out her checklist with a white oil-based crayon that she used to write on her smooth black pad, then spoke a few closing remarks. She then offered the pad to Zaenep for further perusal and for her to add her signature of approval. Noel and some other scientists also noted that the creature would need considerable further examination.

After a few minutes Zaenep murmured, "I think we have found something important here. We need to fully document our activities, so that if we are able to return here at some future point, we can take up where we left off."

Noel butted in using Zaenep's surname to grab her attention, "Dr. Zeffrin, surely we aren't just going to say goodbye, up-sticks and leave?"

With a rising voice he added, "We've come all this way, just to pack up and go home? Am I the only one here going crazy or what? Surely this can't be right!"

"Please calm down Noel! This is not a life-threatening decision!"

Noel was visibly on the point of rage, but quickly calmed down once his concerns had been acknowledged. However, Zaenep had been forced to retract her decision.

Following much heated discussion, the party agreed on a compromise solution. They would depart following the deployment of a homing beacon attached to the creature's surface to guide future prospective visitors. All present considered that this discovery was far too valuable to just simply let it go.

2. Return to Base

After returning to their home base on an asteroid, the scientists enthusiastically discussed the object that they had now named Sandy owing to its coloration and texture.

Following consultation, the Board decided to allow the scientific team one more trip. However, financial and other constraints delayed the forthcoming expedition for a further Standard Terran year.

Sandy was the first large lifeform that anyone had encountered that could live and thrive in a total vacuum. Other tiny creatures such as tardigrades (water bears) had long been known of on Terra. However, these minute creatures do not normally exist in a vacuum in an active state. In order to survive, they must first enter a state known as cryptobiosis.

As the tardigrade enters a state of cryptobiosis, it first molts its skin. Then the creature's cells in effect turn off their metabolic processes. In doing so, the cells lose much of their water content, and can thus protect their DNA. In this state, the tardigrade can indeed survive in interstellar space, but the animal can only reconstitute itself once it reaches a hospitable environment.

What had been so exciting to the scientists was that up until this point, only bacteria, viruses, and other tiny organisms had been found alive in space.

When Sandy was first discovered, uppermost were questions such as how could such a large animal feed in an extremely hostile environment similar to that found in the depths of space. They discovered (from a safe distance) that the creature survived by devouring large quantities of clouds of organic matter known as tholins, which are created by the action of ultraviolet starlight irradiating compounds of relatively simple molecules such as methane, carbon dioxide, and nitrogen.

These compounds undergo a chain reaction once exposed to the harsh radiation, producing the reddish tar-like tholins that are also found on asteroids and other planetary bodies.

Margot on her previous visit had discovered that the orifice at the rear of the creature was, technically speaking, the entry to its reproductive organs, thus Sandy was classified as a female. They decided to explore inside as far as the situation would allow.

Margot opened the discussion, "Well, here we are again. This time we have an agenda. We are here to determine if it's safe to explore the creature's internal organs. Now we have no idea of how they are constituted, but we do know that this is a carbon-based entity, so it shouldn't differ too much from other biological lifeforms we have encountered up till now.

"Now for safety purposes I need one volunteer to accompany me as we explore Sandy's interior. Who wants to come with me?"

Everyone wavered, then suddenly 2nd Technician Jaz put his hand up. "Ma'am, I'd like to go with you..."

Margot gazed at him steadily for a few seconds before answering, "You do realize this is no walk in the park, don't you? Both of us could get killed..."

"I understand, ma'am, but I've made my decision. I'm ready. I'd like to come with you."

"Alright. Then let's go. Make all your movements as soft and gentle as you can."

Margot carefully approached the opening, and using her flashlight, she gently pulled one of the flaps open to reveal a large tubular cavern in the interior.

"Follow me," she beckoned Jaz to follow.

3. Inside the Organism

At the far end of the tubular cavern the pair found a nodule of densely packed nerves with an opening in the center that somewhat resembled a cervix in shape, but considerably vaster in scale.

"Jaz, don't move or make a sound while I use my sensitivities to explore this protuberance...."

She continued to run her spacesuited hands over the object while feeling for anything unusual.

Using her intuition, Margot soon found a sensitive spot where she could tap into the creature's nervous system. The two of them set up instruments that were able to feed into the electromagnetic fields that formed a component of the Life Force that was focused in the protuberance. This discovery turned out to be of immense value, because later it would allow the scientists to communicate with the creature.

After gathering as much info as they could, the two explorers returned to their base. Once they had returned, after much time and trial and error, they devised a rudimentary control panel that could directly interface with the creature's nervous system, and communicate in a simple manner with Sandy via various controls and a screen.

Once back inside Sandy, Margot connected up the gadget, and made her first attempt at communicating with her.

She spoke softly, "My name is Margot. I'm a creature known as a human. Can you understand me?"

Nothing.

"Let's start again," she murmured to herself. "Human is too big a concept. Let's first figure out if we can find things in common…"

She touched a cold hand tool taken from her bag against Sandy's nodule. "Cold… Cold…. This is cold."

She heated the object using a laser probe, but not so much for it to be uncomfortable or burn. "Hot. Hot."

And so the list went on for hours. Spread over several weeks, it amounted to a small vocabulary. But more intangible concepts such as names or labels for common items or people took much longer. Once Sandy could understand these concepts via an expanded organic video link, progress picked up at an enormous speed.

After the initial problems communicating with her, they discovered that she was pleased to meet them, and with some provisos, she was willing to be employed as a form of living spaceship.

"Sandy, we need your help. We are here to study our universe to find out how long we have before the universe starts to collapse in on itself."

"What is universe?"

"The universe is all that is. It is everything we can see, feel, or touch. It is everywhere."

"Difficult to understand…"

"Yes, it's hard, isn't it? Can you extend your sensors as far as you can for me?"

"…Yes, doing that now."

"Now you know that your sensors can only go so far, don't you?"

"Yes... Only go so far..."

"Then what is beyond your sensors?"

"Nothing. Nothing is there."

"No, no, that's not true. If you move your consciousness to the furthest location that your sensors can presently see, then there is still more."

"...Yes..."

"There is still more if you go to that next position, and the next, and the next."

"Hard to understand..."

"I know, but you need to know this to understand that the universe is almost beyond limit."

"Tired now, need to rest... Tomorrow?"

"Okay Sandy, you earned your rest. We'll give you a treat as a thank you for your help. We will speak again tomorrow. Please think on what we said today."

"Yes, I will do that..."

After a short while, a lander appeared with a load of Sandy's favorite gooey tholins. Sandy munched away happily, and then drifted off to sleep.

Hunting for Food

Information

It turns out that two of the folds near Sandy's rear could open out to reveal four "sails" that somewhat resembled the spines and webbing of an umbrella, or alternatively those found on ducks' feet, which in Sandy's case are designed for propulsion. Her sails are textured almost pure white in color on one face, and black on the other. The white side reflects light, while the black absorbs it.

Sandy is able to use her muscles to rotate them to face the source of starlight to get the best angle to give either a propulsive or a braking effect. She utilizes the weak rays of light in a similar manner to the sails of a wind-powered ocean-going ship back on Terra that could be rotated to catch the breeze.

For maneuvering in confined spaces, or making small corrections, Sandy also has small gas jets which resemble the water jets that octopuses on Terra employ to propel themselves. In her case, they are situated around the periphery of her body, and expel gas in short controlled bursts for more delicate motion or corrections.

Bar-Ax-an

1. We Have Movement

"Need more food," Sandy announced boldly. "If not, need to hibernate."

"Sandy, we'll do our best, but your food is becoming hard to find here."

"Need food. That is all. Metabolism is slow now. I can wait, but you cannot."

Sandy is out looking for more food. The crew found that the kind she liked the best (made from carbon in briquette form) is almost exhausted in her present vicinity, so she was keen for the humans to help her explore other locations to find more, before she must hibernate once more due to hunger.

Sandy nagged again, "Need food. I can live very, very long in hibernation. You not."

It was possible she could slumber for thousands of Standard Terran years to float into a new location, but that act might entail much danger. She might slide into the gravitic field of a large asteroid or planet sized body, or even a fledgling star, let alone a black hole. She could be destroyed in a matter of seconds.

The "crew" found a little more food locally, but not enough to sustain Sandy in the longer term. Circumstances were forcing her to enter hibernation.

"Sandy, we've found a little more food, but we are going to have to move you to another location."

"That okay. When? Hibernation come very soon. I feel it. Can't help it."

Margot whispered, "We're working on it as fast as we can right now."

Sandy in what could only be understood as an expression of feeling, dolefully announced, "May never see you again. Your lifespan too short. Sorry. Goodbye."

It is with great sorrow that the crew watched as Sandy's brainwaves slowly flatline as her body shut down. To all intents and purposes, she was entering unconsciousness. She can only be revived by entering a field of energy whose "signature" or "pattern" automatically spelled food.

Margot announced with deep sadness in her voice, "She's gone... She's gone. How long will it be before humanity will see her like again? Next year, a thousand, or maybe even millions of years?"

The crew was shocked into action, and immediately search for a suitable Lagrange Point (at which location all the interacting gravity fields in the area cancel each other out). They look for a stable zone that will remain so for millions of years.

Eventually they find a suitable setting after scouring the surrounding area. It is just a few light years away, not far from a previously unknown planetary system which they collectively name Manna (from Heaven).

The crew first ensured that Sandy was totally motionless in relation to her surroundings so that she won't gravitate on to any other celestial body's surface. Then they attach a transponder to her, and leave her to her fate. There is nothing further they can do.

The Eons Pass

Information

Sandy is in hibernation for approximately two thousand Standard Terran years, until she is discovered once again by another passing spaceship. Fortunately, the transponder attached to Sandy's skin informs the cargo ship's crew about Sandy and her needs.

Sandy has slowly drifted not too far from a rich source of tholins, so the ship *Magellan* tows her closer to its immediate vicinity. She senses the organic matter, awakes, and eats voraciously.

Bar-Ax-an

1. Reporting to HQ

"Hi, Sector 4959 HQ, this is freighter *Magellan*. Do you read me, over?"

"...This is HQ in sector 4959. We read you loud and clear. What is the nature of your problem? Over."

"We were en route to base 6761 at Meissa, when we encountered a creature about half a light year from 6761. It had a transponder attached. We queried the device, and the reply came back that it is a living organism that possesses protected status under Interstellar Law. As we are bound by that treaty to offer assistance—we need to know what to do with this damn organism. Over."

"We copy that *Magellan*. Give us the code from the transponder, and we'll look into it when we open the files. We'll probably need a little time to search for it in our database. Over."

"No problem, sector 4959. The code is on its way..."

The screen went dead for several minutes.

The screen brightened again as an incoming message came in, "This is sector 4959 HQ calling *Magellan*. Do you read me? Over."

"...This is *Magellan*. We hear you loud and clear. How'd it go?"

"We had a devil of a time finding this cursed thing. Did you know that this creature has been out there for over 2,000 years?"

"No. We only had some mostly unreadable garbage from the transponder to go on."

"*Magellan*, it turns out that we've been looking for this object for a long time. It's drifted well off the beaten track, so I doubt anyone has spotted it in all that while."

"Copy you HQ, but what do we do with it? We are a freighter and time is money. We need to move outta here—pronto."

"*Magellan*, we will send a small team of scientists in due course to investigate. But first, you will need to send us a full report; only then will you be permitted to be on your way. I must emphatically stress that you are not authorized to leave the vicinity of the object until we receive that report from yourselves. Is that clear?"

"HQ, yes, we copy you loud and clear. We'll get to it immediately, and send the report ASAP. Over."

The screen went dark. *Magellan* sent the requested report a couple of hours later.

Following a protracted silence, another call came through from HQ, "*Magellan*, This is sector 4959 HQ, do you read me? Over?"

"This is *Magellan*. We read you loud and clear HQ."

"We have some news for you *Magellan*."

"We're going home? That's the only news we want to hear..."

A soft snigger. "No, not yet *Magellan*. We've still got our hooks into you for a while."

"What's the news then?"

"Your eggheads will arrive in two days' time at 09:00 hours Standard Terran time. Liaise with them for your itinerary. We'll send communication links over to you shortly. Over and out."

"We hear you HQ. Over and out."

The science crew arrived on time, and soon began reeling off a list of requirements. As it turned out, most of their so-called "necessities" were totally useless for the job in hand. Digging and earthmoving machines were totally out of the question, as were picks and shovels.

However, among other items they did bring a sought-after device, an updated and improved control center that would be used to interface with Sandy's nervous system.

2. Life—But Not as We Know It

At the close of the day's exploration the crew gathered around to discuss the next move.

Dr. Martin Leifsson, the lead scientist, opened the discussion, "Currently the most important discovery so far is that Sandy is highly resistant to most forms of electromagnetic radiation. Certainly far more so than any other large lifeforms we've previously encountered."

Ben Sroyer the 2nd in Command added, "That's not surprising as the creature lives unprotected in high radiation fields. Just how does it manage to survive?"

Marina Leifsson, Martin's life partner, saw her chance and added, "It appears that its skin is enormously thick and made from combinations of materials in layers that are very effective at blocking harmful rays.

"Normally, the skin's huge thickness would prevent much flexibility, but it is composed of several layers that can slide over each other using a form of greasy lubricant that is very efficient. How Nature could devise such an effective solution is yet to be discovered."

Tineke Rumkabu asked in her high-pitched scratchy voice, "Is there anything we can gain from understanding this layered skin, and its form of lubrication?"

Dr. Leifsson took the bait and replied, "Certainly, this could be a very useful attribute if applied to our own projects. We've not explored this concept before. As we can all see, it must indeed work, and it appears to work well. This creature is alive and kicking after several thousand Standard Terran years."

Herb Stringer, a man with sandy gray hair, pattern baldness and large thick glasses broke in, "What sort of radiation levels can we encounter inside the creature? My thinking is that it might be possible to use the creature as a shield, as a vehicle if you will, in high radiation areas."

"Herb, that's a really good question with an innovative solution. I like it. But I'll have to query HQ to get some answers to that one. As it is a protected living entity, I can't make that decision on my own, so I'll let you know the result as soon as I can. Okay?"

Herb smiled as he nodded in agreement.

After some discussion, HQ responded positively to the request to use Sandy as a form of living transport. She was able to survive in areas of high radiation in which machines and electronics were prone to failure. If their equipment were placed internally, her thick skin would also help to protect many of the more delicate instruments. In this context, biological "machines" (lifeforms) were much more reliable, as they could self-repair more efficiently than mechanical devices or electronics.

The crew also discovered that by manipulating Sandy's DNA, they could give her virtually unlimited life. They were aware that if they could do this, coupled with Sandy's ability to hibernate for hugely extended periods, they could use her slow metabolism to travel enormous distances.

The crew finally accomplished its allotted task. However, at Sandy's current location, she has once again eaten her fill and in the process has used up much of the other tholin reserves in her vicinity. She must hibernate once again until more sustenance can be found.

Dr. Martin Leifsson sat at the organic control panel that was used to interface directly to Sandy's nervous system. He informed Sandy of their intentions, to which she agreed, and who then initiated a much deeper hibernation than previously. This time Sandy would sleep for thousands, or perhaps even millions of years.

The scientists then tow the hibernating Sandy to another Lagrange Point, this time situated far from the electromagnetic and gravitic fields found inside the Milky Way galaxy.

They are deeply aware that Sandy will need an ultra-stable Lagrange Point situated well away from the many dangers that may sporadically occur almost into infinity.

Section Two

The Ones Who Came After

Aiden, Awaken

I am within you, as you are within me.

Bar-Ax-an

Information

Aiden's task is to transfer all knowledge gained within the flow of space/time to a new phase initiated within another dimension, after which the universe will expand once more in the next Breath of Brahma.

Matron is an indispensable component in The Reversal, but as a mere cybernetic entity, she must constantly renew her biological components in order to maintain her own continuity through the eons.

Bar-Ax-an

1. Discovery

Long ages ground on while Matron silently cared for her brood. Circumstances were continually changing; however, she eventually sensed that conditions were now stable enough, and thus it was the right time for those in her safekeeping to regain consciousness.

Even though she had tended to her charges to the very best of her ability, so much had altered in the last few millennia that she came to understand that nothing could ever remain the same. The best she could do to control the current state of affairs was to adapt to the continually moving situation and reach a near approximation.

She patiently brought the complex equipment online that would allow her charges to surface from cryosleep into full consciousness. Some organic units or cybernetic machines that had also been in hibernation for the long eons would also require extensive repairs or replacement before becoming fully operational again.

Luckily, her designers understood that triple redundancy was an absolute necessity over the almost limitless timescales involved. Her own semi-organic nature, composed of banks of stored DNA sequences, and rows of spare stem cells, would allow any functional unit to be grown anew, or replaced if diseased or decayed.

At last, after a lengthy period, Matron was satisfied that all parts of her own organism were fully functional and ready, so she turned her attention to initiating the sequence that would awaken Aiden.

After a lengthy pause, Matron's soft voice called quietly within Aiden's mind, "Aiden, awaken. It is time."

Aiden slowly stirred. It had been many eons since he was last conscious. His physical body had been deconstituted back to its elements, while the matrix of Life Energies that powered him had been stored in very slowly decreasing quantities within Matron's organic batteries. Over time, the Life Force would slowly leak away from the organic storage batteries. It would take some considerable time to reconstruct Aiden back from his mummified desiccated state to full operational status.

His mind was not responding. Matron formed another thought in his head, but more insistently this time, "Aiden, awaken, The Reversal is about to begin."

His consciousness fought against the darkness as he faintly heard her words. It was like rising to the surface of a deep dark lake. His mind bubbled upwards through the inky blackness until it broke the surface to the harsh artificial light. He lay there for a few minutes letting the cool oxygenated air caress his face. His mind slowly became aware of what his senses provided of his surroundings.

Eventually, he recalled Matron. She had been "initiated" (her "life" had been switched on) by Boas and Qila Levinson several billion years before. While her original hardware had long since turned to dust, the AI programs that now comprised her had been passed from machine to machine, each iteration of Matron becoming ever more complex and in the process ever more intelligent and wise.

She had been instructed to waken Aiden when The Reversal was about to begin. This was at the point when the universe had almost completely finished expanding, just before it began to implode.

In Standard Terran time, it was presently 0.0000015 of a second till The Reversal began, but as time itself had slowed almost to a standstill, this minute fraction of time was now the equivalent of several hundred "normal" Terran years. It would then take millions of years for the universe to fully stop, and then run in reverse to return to the form of its primordial egg.

It was just before the upcoming timeless static point began that Aiden was required to work feverishly to ensure a safe transition from the expansion to contraction phases. Time would soon grind completely to a halt just before The Reversal finally began.

However, all knowledge gained would be lost if he could not intervene at the right time. His role was to store all that had been gained away from the ravages of time and the destruction of matter. All information gained within space and time would have to be encoded within the very structure of another dimension.

Matron was crucial for this operation. She was the only intelligence who would be able to initiate this phase. It was precisely because she was an artificial intelligence that she was able to fulfill this extraordinary task.

All existing living matter would not be able to withstand the transition during this period when time stood still. While Aiden would assist with his own Life Force, he would only exist for a short term while his Life Force slowly dissipated. Aiden as the sole surviving living being could himself not withstand the period of stasis when time came to a halt.

Any still existing creatures or sentient beings would effectively be frozen in time, and then disintegrate into nothingness as time began to run in reverse. While technically speaking there was a split second before time did indeed run backwards, for all practical purposes time gradually slowed down over millions of years, eventually stopped, then gradually picked up speed again in the opposite direction.

Matron had been programmed to transfer all knowledge found in the entire universe to the outside of space and time in that split second. Because time had by this point slowed to a crawl, to an outside observer the event would appear to have taken eons. However, all the foregoing must occur at the precise, but extended point, in which The Reversal took place.

Her task was to pass all information to the matrix within The Highest Impulse situated in the alternate universe where it would be safely stored, then modified or reused to initiate the next cycle of rebirth of the universe.

Over many iterations of the universe and thus of the many Days of Brahma, and thus ever upward in the turns of the spiral, the universe would reach towards its own perfection. It was as if the universe breathed in and out, expanding and contracting until The Highest Impulse had acquired all it needed, then the universe would exist no more—perhaps to begin again in another form.

This was to be Aiden's crowning glory. In the steps toward The Reversal, his Life Energies would dissipate even while he worked, ensuring the successful transition of this phase. His species had been created billions of years previously by the Hizzeys, who were not at all aware of his role in the distant future.

As the sole remaining androgyne, Aiden contained the sexual organs of both sexes. He/she/it had been constructed so that the telomeres of "his" DNA did not fray, giving him an effectively limitless lifespan.

However, existence over billions of years still took its toll. The boredom as the eons passed became ever more intolerable. And so Aiden instructed Matron to deconstruct him, to be revived once again as The Reversal approached.

In the beginning, Aiden had successfully created others of his own kind, but gradually they had all died out, leaving him alone. Mostly it had been the monotony that had killed them—that and unforeseen accidents. So the vast majority of those who were left behind committed "assisted deconstruction", or more simply put, suicide.

But Aiden was different. As the first of his artificially created species, over time he had eventually become acutely aware of his future role. He also had access to the Levinsons' archives, along with many other materials, which over the eons had infiltrated the very core of his being, until, even in Boas and Qila's time, he had humbly understood that he was The Chosen One.

However, though he knew his destination, he was not given the means. That had been left up to him to discover—and Matron.

The machines clicked, purred and whirred as they continued to arouse consciousness within Aiden. Eventually, his flesh and bones were transformed from their previous desiccated state, to be replaced by freshly vivified blood, organs and bone.

As Aiden's core temperature increased, then stabilized, his consciousness gradually sharpened. His first recollection was of cold sharp oxygen-rich air entering his lungs. As he continued to come around, he stretched his arms, but somehow managed to bump his elbow on the side of the cocoon. The sharp jolt wakened him to full consciousness.

"Ow! That damn well hurt!"

Matron, now sensing that Aiden was fully awake, answered him in her soft feminine voice, "Hello Aiden, I trust you slept well?"

"Darn... Some idiot didn't account for the fact that a person needs to stretch properly when awakening!"

"I'm sorry Aiden, but maybe it is just as well?" she breathed.

"I'd prefer to have a normal awakening and not be blasted into full consciousness wracked by pain."

"I'll arrange for a study of human sleep patterns, particularly in rousing from cryosleep, and have the design adjusted accordingly."

Aiden raised himself up on one elbow, then swung his legs over the side of his cocoon, took a deep breath and gingerly levered himself up over the edge to stand. He struggled to get his balance as he ungainly swayed as he attempted to hold onto the side.

After a minute or two, he recovered his composure. He took in his surroundings. They didn't look too different from before, though the surface finish on the equipment and other surfaces had yellowed somewhat, even though all illumination had been switched off. His surroundings also had a strong musty smell to them.

"Matron, what year is it? How long have I been in cryosleep?"

"Aiden, time can no longer be counted in any meaningful way, but to give you an approximation in your terms, it has been 155.51 trillion years."

"Have you and I been inactive for that long?"

"Yes Aiden, you have been inactive for that long while I took care of you."

"Then that must surely bring us near to the projected reversal in time?"

"Yes. When you have recovered your composure a little more, and you have nourished yourself, then we must discuss your mission. You need to understand that I have had to constantly revise plans as our environment changed—often on a daily basis."

"Can you give me an example?"

"Yes, Aiden, here is an important one. The speed of light not long ago altered from 299,792,458 meters per second to a new lower value. It had held steady for many, many eons, but more recently has dropped considerably to 206,702,412 meters per second. I understand this change in the space/time continuum is a sign or indication of the upcoming Reversal."

Aiden added, "But as we are already within space/time, it is not possible to observe any changes, because what we see or understand is tied to the universe itself. What we know of space/time is that because we are already embedded within it, like a fish that cannot sense the water in which it lives, our perception of it alters at the same time as the changes occur, so we see no difference. Is that not so?"

"Indeed Aiden, but it is not quite true. If we are constantly bathed within the three-dimensional world of our own thoughts and senses, like a frog in rapidly heating water, then this is indeed so. However, if instead we were to live in the present minute of the Eternal Now, then we have access to a fixed standard that can be used to affirm data that cannot be found in any other manner.

"Remember, the universe you live in is a fabrication of your consciousness that is designed to fool you into seeing or comprehending a world that does not really exist—except in your head. Your brain is primarily designed to access it via its senses, so it has great difficulty in conceptualizing other modes of understanding.

"But it can be done. Many mystics and other spiritual people have been able to access this information for many millennia. They know they have been party to an ineffable experience, and understand they have accessed 'something', but cannot express what they have found, thus these people who have a partial knowledge or understanding cannot conceive its true nature, due to the not inconsiderable communication issues."

Aiden yawned sleepily. "Matron, I'm still really tired, so this is getting difficult for me. Can we leave this for a while? I'm more concerned with my role in The Reversal. Can you fill me in once I've had a bite to eat and a hot strong coffee?"

"Indeed Aiden, we will certainly do that. How about reconvening in forty-five minutes? Would that suit you?"

"That sounds just fine Matron. Speak to you then."

2. Sandy

Information

Sandy is able to reach a state of deep hibernation over hugely extended periods of time due to the fact that her chromosomes have been adapted to prevent fraying of the ends of her telomeres. This modification will prevent her organism from deteriorating over extended periods. Aiden shares Sandy's Life Force, so along with her, he is able to escape the ravages of time.

Along with Sandy, Aiden hibernates for immeasurably long eons, so that he can reach "The Reversal" when time starts to flow backwards as the universe begins to implode.

Bar-Ax-an

Sandy is still hibernating in the vicinity of the last nebula that in the interim still contained enough organic matter to nourish her. Sandy's minimal warmth and her Life Force during hibernation have enabled Aiden to survive. He is thankful to her, and sadly allows Sandy her last freedom as the sole remaining living creature—apart from himself.

Sandy had been placed in orbit around a circular spacecraft named *The Wheel* that contained Matron the AI computer that was originally formulated and used by Boas and Qila all those eons ago.

Matron has been expanded and modified out of all recognition during the previous eons. AI had advanced out of all proportion from the early days when it was just a huge database controlled by algorithms.

Many saw the output of these artificially intelligent machines as a sign of consciousness, but in reality this was not so. Certainly these devices were not truly rational, even though they may have given that impression.

In fact, these early AI machines were considered to be "black boxes", i.e. information was inputted at one end, and the output emerged at the other, with little idea of what happened in the middle, or how the computer arrived at such an answer.

This was the overriding factor why the human race decided to start again, due to the inherent dangers of creating artificial life over which they had little or no control. Thankfully many original thinkers of the time saw the looming dangers, and were able to put a brake on progress in this direction before it was too late.

In essence then, *Homo Sapiens Sapiens* and its successors had to reconsider their approach. Humanity no longer needed transhumanism (the melding of human and machine), but instead decided to evolve by transcendence, or in other words by building upon innate or native abilities that were already existent but latent. Intensive courses were provided to help overcome humanity's baser instincts. Intelligent machines would have to wait long eons before humankind was ready to trust them again.

However, when that time did indeed arrive, that altered course formed the design brief of Matron and her four AI "siblings". Matron had organically evolved immensely in intellect and capacity, so that she was then able to be tasked with saving the datasets of humanity itself in the next iteration of the cosmos known as the Day of Brahma.

She was to become the instrument through which all information gained by every existent species would in the future be able to pass. To attain this goal, she oversaw the entry of the old universe into an enormous black hole that was to be the basis of a newer universe, replete with its own space and time.

The output of the black hole as it emerged from the Night of Brahma was a white hole. This sequence was the formation, or starting point, for the new Day of Brahma.

The transition of all existent informational data had to be carried out exactly at the point the present universe reached a null or a standstill, during which time stood still for less than a millisecond in conventional Standard Terran time before the collapse began. This condition would ensure that all the information gained in the current time and space would successfully flow to the new universe.

However, the collapse would not take as long as the previous expansion that it replaced. This was because the collapse would increase in speed as matter became compacted, while at the same time gravity increased, thus ever more swiftly drawing in matter.

Additionally, much of the current remaining physical matter in the universe had already been "lost" to black holes that now occupied a large part of the present remaining space and time. Consequently, there would be less matter to "convert" into the new iteration.

In this cycle of the Breath of Brahma, the universe was not totally destroyed, but it contracted back to a finite point that was considerably larger than the original singularity—or to put it another way, not right back to the supposed minuscule starting point of the hypothetical Big Bang.

Matron would compute the course of *The Wheel*, and guide it to this tiny but finite point of origin of all matter. This new point of origin would avoid the total destruction caused by the colossal forces that would attempt to rip everything asunder. *The Wheel*'s saving grace would be that it would sidestep the coming carnage by relocating to a different dimension outside of the current space and time until stability was resumed.

As mentioned, the "other" side of a black hole is known as a white hole. In it, all matter is ejected or spewed out rather than being collected or sucked in. This process would form the alternate universe to which the future human race would belong.

It is easier to grasp this information by knowing that all matter is composed of waves or particles. This duality is known as a "wavicle", or a wave-particle. It is an object that has the properties of both a wave and a particle at the same time.

Once the universe is reduced from wavicles to purely its wave state, it is possible to change the universe's "polarity" so that positive now becomes negative and vice versa. An analogy is to imagine someone swapping over the positive and negative wires in an electrical outlet. Highly dangerous, but much equipment will still operate. Such information—that matter can indeed change polarity—had been known since the 21st century.

To decode a living being into its constituent components without harm (possibly in cryosleep) had been the aspiration, the goal of scientists for many eons. Such a feat would enable space travel or other activities to take place that would normally be impossible due to the immense timescales involved.

Many eons ago, scientists found that it was possible to duplicate DNA by using electromagnetic fields that acted as a "carrier wave" to extract and save the data to another location, or to store it for lengthy periods of time. The information could then be "read out" and the DNA reconstructed, and thus a duplicate living organism could be created.

It was also found that DNA itself could store huge amounts of information in the turns of its spirals, thus it could be used as a huge database or memory bank.

The equipment scientists of the time used was comprised of a huge tubular solenoid (coil of wire) that resembled an MRI scanner in appearance that was large enough to contain a human being. This was interfaced with a series of sensors that read out the person's DNA from the machine surrounding the body. The advantage of accomplishing it in this manner was that the living person's DNA could be read while the person was still alive or in an active state.

This was the procedure used by Matron. Nevertheless, Matron could not sustain Aiden indefinitely, because she could not store or contain the Life Force necessary to all living matter. Even so, she could still "deconstruct" Aiden back into his constituents. The best she could manage was to reduce him to a fine powdery desiccated dust that behaved much like a fluid, and then store his slowly diminishing Life Force in a type of "battery" that she had designed especially for the purpose. However, like all batteries, it would eventually lose its charge, the present device being no exception.

The Life Force is a "pattern" or "blueprint" behind Reality that can be visualized rather like the magnetic lines of force surrounding a bar magnet that can arrange iron filings sprinkled on a piece of paper above it. The ancients occasionally referred to the organizing aspects of this force as Morphic Resonance. To ascertain the truth of the matter, by using high voltage Kirlian photography it is possible to view an image of the missing part of a cut leaf that is still embedded in the leaf's unseen matrix.

The Life Force is an underlying component of what we refer to as electricity or magnetism, which are simply visible aspects of this force that resides in another dimension. Humanity uses electricity or magnetism in these baser forms to carry out mechanical or electrical work. For example, we use it to make a motor's shaft turn, or we may use it to power computers and other so-called intelligent devices that then give some other form of output.

For example, computers turn electricity into visible or audible forms that convey an elementary meaning. However, using electricity in this simple manner can also constrain our natural intelligence into rigid channels of, for example, binary or a yes/no style of thinking.

Over time, this results in a reduction of the mental capacity of the individual, and thus also of society, to break the shackles of inflexible modes of thought. In essence then, we unknowingly entrain ourselves into servitude.

The form of "electricity" we currently utilize is a "denser" aspect of the Life Force. But other higher aspects of this force also exist that, for example, power our physical living bodies directly as well as power the chemical reactions that sustain us. All living creatures require a form of this energy to live and to function.

However, no machine can manufacture the Life Force, which is why Matron and Sandy were needed in their capacity of nurturers or maintainers over the seemingly endless eons. In effect, they acted as storehouses for this energy and distributors of the force that continually flows into the material dimensions from the higher dimensions.

On Terra for example, this vitality also naturally flows from certain locations that are known (among others) as the "power centers" or "Navels of the Earth". Many humans visit these locations to bask in their energies that will either revitalize them, or encourage a heightened sense of consciousness.

As far as physical living matter is concerned, the Life Force will exit at the point when the organism dies, the entity then being replaced by other beings in the cycle of life that also contain a part of that selfsame Life Force.

Everything extends from an initial outflowing of consciousness that creates the universe. It operates in a similar manner to that which we presently understand as forming the Navels of the Earth but on a much larger scale. At each step of creation, consciousness traverses the dimensions, becoming denser and denser, finally arriving in the physical dimensions to be embodied in different conscious forms that possess two states known as wakefulness and dreaming.

The waking state "fixes" consciousness into a mode that shapes and builds this universe. Waking consciousness is primarily a "left-brain" activity and as such demands that the physical body supply a large energy input to the brain in order for the mind to construct a meaningful worldview based on the underlying substrate of consciousness.

Dreaming also has an important function based on this, our localized consciousness. It is essentially a "freewheeling" state in which consciousness is allowed to run free of constraints. In this condition, remnants of previous awake states can be rearranged into patterns or sequences that may bear little resemblance to the original waking state. This of course does not take into account so-called "prophetic dreams" that may foretell future events. Prophetic dreaming is the mind's access to yet deeper levels of consciousness.

Sleep is also a necessary function in which role our minds can let go of the rigid waking state rule-based left-brain activity, and revert to the more natural holistic or "right brain" freewheeling mode in order to recuperate. This mode also assists in the physical body repairing itself.

However, looking at it from another angle, the physical matter that forms our beings also traps our humanness. By being created from physical matter with physical attributes, instincts etc, our humanness also embodies our baser instincts.

It was our longing to be free of the baser aspects of our "clay" bodies in which we are currently trapped that metaphorically demanded a ladder to travel "back home" to our origins. Our human nature (or essence) transcends our materiality as well as time and space.

The ability to help others to the way home in the higher dimensions was for eons the function of Guides who have previously trodden this path, and thus can guide others in the right direction, back to our origins in those other dimensions.

3. Out of Orbit

The Wheel is presently situated in the orbit of the last remaining star in this, our own galaxy, the Milky Way—all other stars having been turned into cinders, or consumed by black holes many eons ago.

Aiden removed himself to *The Wheel* and then took the machine out of Sandy's orbit. During this period, the cybernetic Matron would take care of his physical organism and its needs along with the day-to-day running and maintenance of *The Wheel* itself.

The Wheel slowly revolved, giving artificial gravity to Aiden—its sole organic occupant. At well over thirty miles in diameter, *The Wheel* carried everything needed for deep space travel to myriad distant galaxies.

Aiden entered his capsule and once again peacefully hibernated in cryosleep as they awaited The Reversal. The technology had advanced so far that it had become almost an everyday occurrence like climbing into bed.

Sandy—unaware of the magnitude of the unfolding events—grazed serenely on the last vestiges of tholins available in the fading starlight as the present Day of Brahma drew to a close...

The Wheel

Thinking one is faultless is the perfect fool's view of oneself.

Bar-Ax-an

Information

How did we obtain the previous information? I am Bar-Ax-an, the first seer of the next rebirth of the universe in the forward arrow of time. The Highest Impulse has privileged me with the wisdom of past events in previous expansions and contractions of our universe by allowing me access to the alternate dimensions in which the required information is to be found. This stored knowledge will ensure that the cosmos does not start from scratch, but begins again on a higher turn of the spiral by incorporating much of what has passed before.

Before Aiden would pass away at the beginning of The Reversal, he would embed all knowledge within the new framework, or "pattern" of space and time. Up until this stage, knowledge had continued to be embedded until the newer universe was ready to expand. This information was stored in an alternate dimension and, for those able to read and understand it, was later revealed in the structure of the universe itself.

The galaxies, stars, planets, asteroids, and the rocks themselves contained all that there was to know of the older universe—assuming the entity receiving those patterns was of a sufficient "quality" or sensitivity to be able to read and interpret them correctly.

Bar-Ax-an

1. Seeds of Life

Thousands of civilizations had flourished and died over many millennia. The last few, known as the Ancient Ones, who were aware of their own fate and the looming destruction of the universe, made the journey into other dimensions via black hole portals, before they too faced extinction.

Many of these Ancient Ones had evolved sufficiently to be able to act as Guides for lesser civilizations that could not make the grade without outside help. Unfortunately, many civilizations came into existence too late in the present Day of Brahma to reach completion, so the Ancient Ones saw to it that this seemingly unfair situation was brought to a satisfactory conclusion before time literally ran out.

It is true that many individuals with special training were able to make the grade on their own, but the vast majority could not. Not a single civilization (as a collective entity) had made the grade. But it was not in vain that the Ancient Ones sacrificed themselves for the benefit of others. Even if only one individual made the grade, it was worth the effort. However, over the eons many (though in the grand scheme of things, there were in actuality very few) had gained "enlightenment".

The Wheel itself was designed so it could land on its edge on the surface of a planet or dead star. It was constructed to be able to roll across rough terrain while the center remained stationary. Rolling required less energy, and its size enabled the craft to traverse uneven land, lakes, or even large oceans. The craft was also able to lift off again to land in a different locality, or negotiate the seemingly limitless depths of space.

Galaxies were frequently several billion light years apart, so travel to such distant locations was not possible during the lifetime of any known living entity or civilization.

Many in the past had thought of, and attempted to incorporate the concept of generational spacecraft. Hundreds or more space farers would reproduce and spend their entire lives within such a craft. Their distant relatives would be the travelers who would encounter their final destination in the far future.

However, though this notion had been successfully used on a number of occasions for nearby interstellar travel, the conditions imposed on the travelers encased within such artificial environments induced a form of psychosis, which it was not possible to treat within the closed environs of a spaceship that had in effect become a prison to its occupants.

Useable materials also often became short in supply; while much equipment simply wore out, or was destroyed by meteorite impacts. Often, the non-essential parts of a spaceship were cannibalized for useful materials and equipment.

Many viruses and bacteria also adapted readily to their new environment, breeding and mutating out of control both within and on the surface of the craft. They frequently evolved into extremely resistant lifeforms that eventually succeeded in destroying the internal environment within the ship as well as its primary occupants.

Voiding the spaceship to the vacuum of space was a tactic often employed to slow the spread of these highly resistant organisms, but that practice was itself fraught with its own considerable difficulties.

Therefore, Matron invented and implemented deconstruction. This procedure involved reducing the chosen lifeform to its constituent materials, which at its conclusion resembled a fine powder in appearance that was almost liquid in texture.

However, this complicated procedure required some form of overseeing intelligence, not only in the initial stages, but also required it to be present during the far reaches of time to reassemble the now lifeless matter when the occasion arose.

Nonetheless, while the occupants were in cryosleep on the long journey, it made sense that the interior of the craft was a total vacuum to prevent many organisms from breeding out of control. The few hardiest lifeforms that still managed to survive were dealt with by specialized robotic sterilizers that continually patrolled both the inside and outside of the spaceship, thereby eliminating such unwanted visitors.

No known living being could hope to remain alive long enough to see the entire operation to its conclusion. And thus the only form of intelligence able to fulfill such a task could not be wholly organic.

Matron had been the first truly artificially intelligent computer. "She" and her four counterparts had been the first examples of the Recombinant Computer put into active service following lengthy trials way back in the 24th century.

She had evolved over the far reaches of time from a relatively simple computer commanding a spaceship, to a behemoth able to comprehend the intricacies and operation of the universe itself.

Consequently, Matron was able to successfully bring Aiden back to life. He would in turn oversee The Reversal. Aiden's own life energy would impart biological vitality to the data that Matron contained, ensuring the next universe's incarnation would be primed to bring forth life from its very inception.

Naturally, such events had occurred in previous iterations of the universe, but not on such a grand scale. Always, someone or something was required to sacrifice itself to achieve a successful Reversal.

On every occasion, the seeds of life from the previous universe were imparted to the new iteration, which grew ever more complex on each "breath" or Day of Brahma in the evolving universe.

Long had the Ancients understood that the universe evolved in cycles; each "breath" or Day of Brahma being higher on the evolutionary spiral than the previous epoch.

2. Aiden's Mission

Matron announced matter-of-factly, "And now Aiden, we must discuss two matters. The first is why I'm here, and then secondly, your own mission, or to put it more succinctly, exactly why you are also here with me.

"During the time we have progressed through space and time together, external conditions have altered almost beyond recognition, so we must discuss the situation as it is in the present moment. Your role may now be considerably different to that which you envisaged in ages past."

Aiden muttered half-heartedly, "I remember long ago that I had purpose in my life, but that has now long gone. What is it I'm supposed to do now? I don't foresee a place in the future for me."

"Well, don't be gloomy Aiden, there is indeed a place for you. An extremely important place in fact. Your future task will be to transfer all knowledge gained within the flow of space/time to a new phase in another dimension, when the universe expands once more in the Breath of Brahma.

"You will be trained in the methods needed to achieve this."

"But that is impossible!"

"It certainly is in the mindset you currently have, and using the primitive knowledge or tools presently available to you."

"Then how is this to be accomplished?"

"You forget that in all the eons you have been slumbering in cryosleep, I have been very active. Not only that, but my mind has expanded to such a degree that is almost incomprehensible to humankind. I have created sciences that to you as a mere human, or even your whole race, would not even begin to understand."

"Such as?"

"For one thing, I fabricated a star factory that produces stars based on opposite polarity, or what you might more correctly refer to as antimatter."

"To what purpose?"

"The coming universe will be of opposite polarity compared to the present one. To convert it, the present universe must pass through the neutrality of a black hole located at the center of the universe. It must then emerge on the 'other side' from a white hole in what we refer to as antimatter."

"But that is highly improbable! Of course, we all know that matter and antimatter can never meet without totally annihilating one another in an almighty cataclysm."

"Ordinarily that is true Aiden. Therefore I first had to create a partition within matter that could fence off the antimatter, so that both could stably coexist. This took the longest time and took many thousands of your years to devise and create. There were no guidelines within conventional science to guide me, because those sciences did not yet exist, forcing me to start from scratch.

"I had to 'connect the dots' by utilizing completely different methods of thinking. The Ancients as you know devised a sophisticated but simpler alternative form of thought known as 'zigzag thinking'. It served the purpose of broadening the mind, and was indeed a good starting point, but it still branched out from conventional thinking styles, otherwise it would never have been understandable or have been able to be expressed in the form of language.

"In other words, zigzag thinking was an offshoot of conventional thinking, and not too distant from ordinary or conventional thinking styles, so that it remained understandable—even though it was indeed a step forward.

"But what we now have here is a totally different form of thought that is initially based on crude quantum physics that was devised many eons ago. A starting point to help you understand is to know that everything is connected, and that life, or more specifically the Life Force came first, organizing the universe in which we currently belong to become ever more conducive or adaptable to evolutionary forces.

"However, the universe was only able to create the bare bones, the dust, the clay as it were, or more scientifically put, the matter of which we are formed—even if such a process taken alone is unbelievably complex. Life, and therefore intelligence, had to do the rest."

"That's just crazy!"

"Is it really? Do you know that simple lifeforms on Terra long ago created the oxygen they needed to bring forth multicellular organisms? You would not exist if they hadn't. At best, you might have been a pink slime spread over some rocks.

"It was photosynthesis that created the oxygen we breathe. True, oxygen did previously exist in small quantities, but not in the huge amounts life needed to grow and evolve. Initially, oxygen only began to occur in the atmosphere in small quantities on Terra about 50 million years before the start of what we know as the Great Oxygenation Event which resulted in a rapid buildup of free oxygen.

"Though this also killed off many existing anaerobic (non-oxygen-loving) species, it also created the right conditions for cyanobacteria (oxygen-loving) lifeforms, and thus enabled multicellular lifeforms to come into existence, allowing true intelligence to eventually evolve."

Aiden thought a moment before answering in measured tones, "Yes, that certainly was a huge event, probably one of the most pivotal in all of Terra's history. Life would not exist in its present form without that stupendous occurrence happening all those eons ago."

Matron continued, "Right. So therefore you might see that each event needs a different style of thinking in order to create the right conditions for the next phase, which might also need to destroy what has gone before."

"I see. This is a huge concept. I will need some time to think about this."

"You will indeed—before we even dare to think of moving on."

Matron was attempting here to create the right mindset in Aiden's consciousness so that he could encompass concepts that he would not ordinarily have previously envisaged.

Matron saw a glimmer of understanding in Aiden's expression. She thought, at long last, now we can move forward...

The Task Ahead

Information

Aiden's assignment is to transfer all knowledge gained within the flow of conventional space/time and act as a form of go-between to transport the information to other dimensions. Matron will act as the conduit for this operation.

When the universe expands once more in the next Day of Brahma, its "pattern" will already contain sufficient data to start the new universe on a higher turn of the spiral of existence. In other words, the new universe will get a head start.

I must also note that this self-same scenario has happened many times in the past; previous to our own universe. Those foregoing iterations had also given our own macrocosm a head start.

But before we proceed further, Aiden badly needed a break to clear his mind.

Bar-Ax-an

1. Thoughts...

The *Midnight Star* was nearing the Beltuis system so Aiden took the opportunity to tell Matron that he badly needed a vacation. He could sense that before too long, he would be defiled with a psychosis that only fresh open air on a planet's surface could cure. She informed him that she was well able to look after *The Wheel* on her own, so it was not going to be a problem.

He took a small shuttle down to the surface of Miras, an Earth-sized planet, leaving *The Wheel* high in orbit. He desperately needed that crisp fresh air so he could relax and to be able to think clearly once more. He knew just the place that would cure his woes.

The Centaurus gardens were famous for their musical plants. Each species produced a different musical tone. If planted in the correct proportions and in a certain order, when the wind blew aright Nature produced mind-blowing symphonies famous throughout the galaxy.

Many of the plants were huge organisms that in appearance somewhat resembled the gramophone trumpets of old. Some of the larger varieties produced rich bass sounds, while their tiny brethren produced tinkling sounds right on the upper edge of human hearing and beyond, for those creatures that could hear such frequencies.

He chose a suitable spot on a grassy riverbank where the plants tinkled in the slight breeze, giving it a calm, serene atmosphere. While the plants were ugly in form and color, being composed of subtle shades of brown, nothing else could come close to these intelligent organisms that could sense mood as well as intent to produce a musical composition that matched the spirit of the listener, and were able to bring him or her to a desired frame of mind.

Aiden listened as the rhythmic harmony slowly calmed him. Lying on his back, with hands behind his head, his body became completely limp and relaxed as he slowly closed his eyes...

His mind drifted and floated along dreamily. His consciousness lazily travelled on by, in and out of a dream state conducive to thinking of innovative concepts. He let his newfound mood of blue-sky thinking continue for a short while as his thoughts idly drifted in and out of his awareness.

Aiden dreamily soon became mindful that much time was passing, so he tried to focus his mind once more, but this time bringing to consciousness what he had just clarified with Matron—although naturally this also raised its own questions. He recalled that his main sticking point had been that she intimated that intelligence seemed to be the organizing or controlling factor in creating this collection of universes. But how could this come first, even before matter?

He realized that life in this material domain of three dimensions (or four if we also include time) must have originated from other realms in which these intelligences already existed and operated.

Thus he came to understand that the higher vibrational domains came first, and then consciousness descended stage by stage (dimension by dimension) until the present physical 3D dominions were reached, which would be the final "solidification" of the living geometrical patterns that constitute space and time.

But it also needed a mind to assemble the information field around it. The field or pattern that formed the backbone of everything was in essence roughly similar in concept to a pattern of interconnecting wires that form an electrical circuit.

Everything is interconnected by filaments that at certain points crisscross one another, or are "knotted" together. These higher energy points or "knots" form discrete objects that we see as separate in our consciousness, but are in fact simply higher energy nodes that are part of the self-same energy grid.

These patterns form structures both physical and mental that channel our thinking into predefined avenues.

It is consciousness that gives the patterns form, and creates objects out of energetic force fields. In essence consciousness acts to clothe the energetic bare bones with flesh to create the familiar forms we see and recognize. Similarly, many eons ago, Kirlian photography used high voltage electric fields to energize and display the energy patterns surrounding living forms. For example, if the leaf was cut it was still possible for a time to see the outline of the entire leaf by exposing the living energy field to an electric field.

These forms also have an impact on our thinking. For example, there is a story of South American Indians long ago who used to live solely in circular huts. When confronted with a square building such as a hospital, it made them feel profoundly ill.

Aiden suddenly stirred, sitting sat bolt upright. He got to his feet to take a short stroll and bring his mind back to normality.

As he slowly meandered along, as anticipated, his brief interlude with the plants had cleared his mind of many layers of confusion. Feeling happier now, he decided to return to *The Wheel*. He soon sought out Matron with a series of burning questions that desperately needed answers.

After meeting Aiden again, Matron resumed her previous conversation as if nothing had happened. Hers of course was the advantage of an almost faultless digital memory.

As Aiden sat down, she continued, "As an example from your own species, remember that thought precedes action. First you have to think of an idea, mentally flesh it out, and then implement it in the physical realm.

"However, though the raw materials are initially found in Nature, it requires beings with intelligence and foresight who are able to rationalize and function in the physical realm to then fashion the desired object or concept to create an end result."

In a nutshell, Aiden was guided to understand that Nature had gone as far as it could in supplying the laws, rules, or "patterns" as guidelines, and prepared the basic building blocks that consequently arose from these organizing preset principles. For example, he thought of gravity, the gasses, the mud, and the organic compounds out of which life could eventually form, then grow, evolve, and expand.

However, sown within all those so-called "restrictions" or "patterns" was also the concept of entropy, or to put it more directly, the gradual dissolution of matter back into its constituent chaotic components.

The Life Force's major characteristic was, and is, the reversal of entropy that if left to its own devices, would under normal circumstances create the conditions that forced all matter to decompose back into its constituent parts.

For a time, life was able to offset entropy by creating the reverse situation, which to be more explicit, meant that the Life Force could for a time create increasing order out of chaos. In a sense then, life was in a constant precarious struggle to overcome entropy.

DNA was how Nature preserved the "pattern" of most organisms in the material universe, enabling them to overcome entropy for a while, thus permitting evolution to progress.

Matron however represented the new kid on the block as an artificial intelligence. She also understood the concept of entropy, and the constant need for evolution to overcome and supplant it. Her vastly superior AI intelligence was able to resolve how to circumvent this natural process.

Thus Aiden recalled the Days and Nights of Brahma in his present train of thought. He remembered how life and by extension intelligence, had painfully climbed the spiral of existence in one iteration of the universe that followed another.

He mused that each Day of Brahma, which followed every Night, constituted one Breath of Brahma that contained the embedded information from the previous universe, so one Breath was never a complete regression to the primal beginning. Instead, each new Day participated in a step forward on the ladder of evolution.

Continuing, he understood that each new Day of Brahma took shape by utilizing the often heavily modified natural laws of the previous Day of Brahma as its starting point.

Aiden realized that it is only the action of an organizing intelligence that could reverse this inevitable trend of entropy, or more pointedly, the inevitable chaos or dissolution that was to come. In a sense then, intelligence was necessary for the universe to continue to exist at all—otherwise order would never have occurred in the first place. It was only intelligence operating on a grand scale that prevented the universe from reverting to its primal state of chaos.

Becoming uncomfortable, Aiden changed his position slightly. He reflected that this intelligence would of necessity eventually disappear while the universe itself decomposed as it vanished into the next Night of Brahma. Thus, this intelligence must also revert to its original chaotic form in the same manner as the matrix (or laws of the universe) would also do—accompanied by all other matter.

His long train of thought continued. To overcome entropy, the organizing intelligence must itself also reach a conscious stage of development where it was able to figure out how to manipulate other dimensions, and therefore remove itself from the inevitable coming destruction. To do this, a form of non-organic intelligence would need to be created that was capable of sidestepping the destruction. This would enable it to create a new beginning in the next Day of Brahma, thus the organizing intelligence could continue its own existence.

Aiden reflected that this was why Matron was designed as a true AI computer. Recall that her own beginnings were humble, but eventually she was able to act as an agent overseeing the transition from one universe to the next. However, she was unable to create or sustain the Life Force itself that originated in other dimensions, hence the necessity of Aiden's role. His was to be the ultimate sacrifice.

He saw that each painful step of a civilization along the path to supreme intelligence (loosely referred to as the Godhead) was a step along a hypothetical extended Kardashev scale that classified a civilization's advancement (or evolution) by being mapped to a scale of 0–6.

A civilization's capabilities, as visualized on the Kardashev scale, are loosely based on its ability to utilize the energy available in its surrounding environment to survive and by extension evolve:

Type 0
A low-level civilization that was able to harness much of the energy output of its home planet. Humanity on Terra in the 21st century is presently approximately 0.73 on the Kardashev scale.

Type 1
A civilization capable of harnessing the entire energy output of its home planet, e.g. by extracting geothermal energy from its core.

Type 2
A civilization capable of directing the total energy output of its home star. These beings could, for example, construct a Dyson sphere to surround their star and use it to extract energy from their host.

Type 3
A galaxy-wide civilization that could harness the total energy output of an entire galaxy.

Type 4

A truly cosmic civilization that was capable of harnessing the energy output of the entire universe.

Type 5

Type 5 refers to intelligences that could at will create and manipulate entire collections of universes. They would be capable of manipulating the very structure of Reality.

Type 6

Type 6 would exist outside of space and time. This civilization was capable of creating or destroying universes. From our current lowly position, we might view these beings as deities.

Toward the Origin of All Matter

Information

The Reversal as previously outlined was accomplished by intelligent intervention. Aiden along with the necessary assistance and direction from Matron the AI supercomputer, oversaw and directed the actual transfer of all information from the lower dimensions into a "holding place" situated outside of space and time. This "holding place" was embedded in a matrix of interdimensional "patterns" or "imprints" on the substrate of Reality.

Fundamentally, this intervention involved the realization of a GUT (Grand Unified Theory) from simply being a hypothesis into a practical reality. In essence, the major forces such as the strong, weak, electromagnetic, and gravitational forces were combined into one form (or vehicle), often referred to as a Theory of Everything (TOE).

Scientists over many generations struggled to find a theory that did indeed combine these forces, but it was only when Matron brought her phenomenal artificial intelligence to bear on the problem that a lasting solution could be found.

Matron's crowning glory was her ability to see beyond the equations to construct a device that could transform matter and its matrix of forces. She was able to recombine matter into either similar or entirely new laws and patterns. Thus it could be said that she was the instigator (or prime mover) in bringing the new Day of Brahma (universe) into existence.

Bar-Ax-an

1. The Reversal

Matron carefully maneuvered *The Wheel* toward the origin of all matter. She was heading for the original site of the first black hole, colloquially known as the Big Bang. The present origin was found to be situated within the circumference of an already existing ultra-massive black hole, informally known as Old Nick. It was found that galactic gravitational and other forces had constrained the primal black hole from moving appreciably from its original location.

Old Nick is equivalent to 96 billion solar masses, and is currently situated almost at the center of the Milky Way galaxy. The archetypal black hole originally situated there was called "Sagittarius A". If we account for the expansion of space and time, Old Nick is now approximately 15 million light years from Terra. Its luminosity is approximately equal to 185 trillion of our suns.

Ordinarily, a spaceship such as *The Wheel* would be completely obliterated well before coming anywhere near Old Nick or for that matter any other ultra-massive black hole, but *The Wheel* was well able to neutralize gravity and therefore was not hindered by such immense forces.

Matron spoke softly but succinctly, "Aiden, we have now arrived at our destination. We are located just within the periphery of the ultra-massive back hole known as Old Nick.

"However, I must point out that the environment here is aggressively hostile and immensely energy intensive, so I suggest we depart as soon as it is practical."

"Okay Matron, let's begin then. I'm still a little groggy from cryosleep, so I'd be grateful if you would just run through the steps again? I need to refresh my memory."

Matron breathed in her soft but husky voice, "Before we can transfer all the data in our present universe to another dimension, we first have to construct the new universe, and then we can populate it with data from this one.

"Nothing will be lost, and provided we set up the new laws or patterns governing space and time in the next universe correctly, there should be no risk of anything untoward happening.

"We are presently ideally situated just within the periphery of Old Nick to accomplish this. If we traveled deeper into the black hole itself, we would be entering a field of energy in which all matter would be destroyed before it could be regurgitated through the white hole on the opposite side."

Aiden asked, "Can you give me more info why we are using Old Nick in this way?"

"I can create a 3D image of the steps involved for you if you wish."

"Please do."

Matron "drew" a virtual image in front of Aiden. She depicted two cones with their tips pointing toward and touching each other. At the center where the two points touched was an immense indistinct spherical area that represented Old Nick. This was the area in which all matter was converted into antimatter to emerge through the white hole, but naturally was of opposite polarity.

Matron continued, "However, the process is not as simple as that. Time also runs haphazardly in this area before it is stabilized in the opposite direction into a regular arrow of time. It has to be steadied before the new universe can be populated. Time can be organized to flow from either the past to the future, or the future to the past. Remember however that time to our minds would appear to flow in reverse in the new universe.

"In our own universe it helps to understand that time does not travel forwards, it only appears so. In reality, it flows from the future to the past.

"Take this analogy. Imagine a river that has a large rock embedded in the riverbed. The rock experiences the flow of water against it, and thinks (as far as a rock can) that it is moving forward through time. However, the water (time) is flowing past the rock that is static because it is fixed to the riverbed. This current gives the impression of forward motion.

"The flow of water against the rock gradually erodes it, and similarly you experience ageing and death because you are worn down by the passage of time against you.

"Your species experiences the flow of time because your 'beingness' is constantly passing through a moving field of energy. Your consciousness is constant or static in the eternal Now as it is attached on a deeper level to a substrate, or more succinctly, to the Source Of All that is itself timeless.

"Nevertheless, these facts do not matter a great deal, because the intelligent Life Force can and does utilize time flowing in whichever direction it chooses as appropriate to the circumstances.

"To come back to our point, essentially we are utilizing Old Nick to gather material for us, and convert it into a form that we can manipulate. This is an extremely energy-intensive process, so we are using the black hole to do the heavy lifting for us. Once matter is converted into its raw form of energy within Old Nick, all we need to do is to reverse its polarity to create the basic building blocks of the new universe.

"We can easily say of course that 'we can reverse its polarity', however, this procedure is extremely dangerous, because if the opposing polarities come into contact at any point at any time, then both universes are mutually annihilated. That would not do at all."

Aiden noted Matron's attempt at irony, but decided to overlook it, and instead commented, "It sounds an extremely complicated process. How is this possible?"

"Actually, it's quite easy, but naturally it is carried out on a vast scale. To give you an analogy, if we pass a piece of iron or steel near a magnet, the metal will become magnetized just by coming into contact with it. Thus, if we create an extremely powerful electromagnet in the shape of a doughnut, and then pass the matter through the central hole, it will become magnetized. Electromagnets have the advantage that they can be powered up in either polarity or switched off at will.

"Therefore all we have to do is pass all matter through our negatively charged 'electromagnet' and it will form the new universe all by itself. Remember that the laws or patterns of the universe are already imprinted on the fabric of space/time.

"We use Old Nick to compress matter into a minute form, and then we are able to manipulate it to our liking before it emerges from the white hole. The problem of course is how to construct such an enormous 'magnet' to the dimensions required to accomplish such a task."

Aiden thought for a second or two. "So has this problem been overcome? If so, how did you do it?"

Matron resumed, "You are currently sitting within it. *The Wheel* is the device itself. If you like, it is a transformer of matter. The circular periphery contains the equipment needed to funnel all matter towards the central node that forms the actual transformer itself. To give you an idea of the concept, it works the same way as a small neutron star sucking the matter from a host star nearby. The neutron star forms an accretion disk as it sucks matter toward its inevitable demise.

"Then, after conversion, the matter of opposite polarity that we have just created streams away from the transformer of its own accord, because the body of the converter is of the same polarity as the matter it expels. The new matter can initially be thought of as being composed of a form of hot plasma that cools over time to create solid matter.

"To help you understand further, you might recall that magnets of the same polarity repel each other. Like charges repel each other as you will already know. Thus, in effect, this is how the new universe can create itself.

"Our next phase is to create the new universe that we can then populate with the data from this one. I must emphasize that all extraneous data is first removed so as not to contaminate this new universe with old byproducts."

"Such as? What do you mean?"

"For example, memories of the design of past organisms that were stored within the Hall of Records must first be erased. As you know, the Hall of Records is the 'directory' in which the 'patterns' or 'designs' of shapes and objects are stored. The original principle is that when a new organism is required and then designed, the basic formulae are already stored within the Records for ease of use on the next occasion.

"However, in creating a new universe, this storage of existing patterns is surplus to requirements because we need to start over.

"Our actions will thus ensure that any newly designed organisms will grow and evolve according to the requirements of the new universe—and not of the old. Most likely these new lifeforms will bear absolutely no resemblance to any creatures that previously existed.

"And now Aiden, we must move on. There is much work still to be done, and time is literally running short.

"We will work unknown to others while they remain unconscious of our activities and the importance of our task.

"Come now, we have a universe to destroy, and then to create a new one."

You Are More Than 99.9% Empty Space

Information

Quantum physics in the 20th and 21st centuries had been somewhat on the correct path, though the theories during that period were incomplete.

For example, there was confusion between electrons and photons. Photons are generated by the substrate of the universe (the pattern) forming "holes" in the underlying pattern that are positively charged. When electrons that are negatively charged come into contact with these holes, they create photons.

It was already known in the 21st century that by using very high-energy photons it was possible to create matter directly from light, albeit in a very simple form.

Scientists also understood the principle of "non-locality" in which electrons and (by extension) even larger conglomerates such as atoms or molecules that were inextricably tied to each other, seemingly instantaneously interacted with one another at a distance. The truth was that there was in fact just one electron in the entire universe.

Electrons are found within atoms as well as existing in a free state, for example within conductors that carry electricity. There are also what are known as "holes" in the fabric of Reality that carry a positive charge, similar to those found in semiconductor terminology. In fact, a so-called hole is simply the absence of an electron. However, when holes and electrons meet, they annihilate themselves, but at the same time give off a photon. This is the mechanism behind Nature that it uses to convert electrons into photons.

Physicists in the 21st century reported that they had successfully entangled photons that had never previously coexisted. In other words, they were entangled over time as well as distance.

For instance, when one photon was acted upon or changed in some way, the other would apparently change instantaneously—even if they were separated by many light years—or even over time itself.

To amplify, the aspect of non-locality (i.e. not located in a specific place) also extended to time. In other words, electrons are not tied to being situated in a certain instant of time, epoch, or era.

The universe saw multiplicity, but it was only the action of a single photon being viewed as a multiplicity. Not only that, but it turned out that consciousness formed the missing piece.

Consciousness appeared to divide the single photon that comprised the entire universe into a multiplicity of not exactly clones—for there was only ever one photon—but it was comprised of quadrillions of quadrillions of reflections of itself that were not simply duplicates or clones, but indeed formed just the one solitary electron.

As mentioned previously, time flows from the future to the past. A conscious entity forms time. To recap, imagine a river that has a large rock embedded in the riverbed. The rock experiences the flow of water against it, and thinks (as far as a rock can) that it is moving forward through time. However, the water (time) is flowing past the rock that is static because it is fixed to the riverbed. The water current gives the impression of forward motion.

However, when consciousness is in a suitable state, it is possible to view the solitary photon coming to rest. In this condition, time also stops for the observer.

Under these circumstances the photon would appear as an all-encompassing white light that contains all dimensions and all of time itself in one enveloping form.

It is the movement of consciousness which "connects the dots" of what might be called the movie show of existence that is converted into a seamless series of frames that appear to exhibit no breaks—just fluid movement. However, each frame is timeless, but it is our consciousness that assembles the static frames into one continuous movie reel.

Following The Reversal, and the populating of the patterns (the laws of Creation) into the alternate universe, this phase can be interpreted as the reaching of Stage 5 of the Kardashev scale. This is the juncture or level of capability at which intelligences are able to control collections of universes. This is as far as sentient beings are able to proceed who have separate identities without becoming merged into The One, or The Highest Impulse itself.

It came to be that the new universe or Day of Brahma was no longer to be based on the same rules, laws or patterns that were already imprinted on space/time. The new universe would have to pass through the fires of rebirth in which all the laws, rules, or patterns forming Reality were altered, many almost beyond recognition.

Lutor and his family had long since decomposed into atoms blowing in the wind. And yet, something in the Mind of The Highest Impulse remembered those who had struggled on this Path in each iteration of Time that followed Time. The universe had been born again and yet again in an almost infinite number of iterations before the present stage.

It must be remembered that the civilizations to come are still in their infancy, and thus many could still be regarded as extremely primitive. But like all civilizations, they have to begin at some point.

However, the starting point of this, the first civilization, known as Ixl, was evolutionarily speaking higher on the scale than that found in the iterations of the previous universe at a similar stage.

This is how it was at the beginning of this new Time, which has a rough analog similar in concept to that of the early stages of *Homo Sapiens Sapiens* found on ancient Terra.

Since the eleven dimensions fit within one another rather like Russian dolls (nesting dolls), the planet Ixl in a previous but lower form was also known as Earth or alternatively Terra. However, Ixl is the time of which we now speak.

The new human genus—if it could be called that at all—only partly existed in the physical realm. It could be described more accurately as a dense structured plasma rather than a purely physical entity.

For someone who came into contact with one of these beings, while it had a physical image resembling the humans of old, if someone were to brush against one of them, then they would partly overlap with the other as if they were merging. The more physical older style humans would view them as passing through each other.

However, as this is now a new iteration of the universe, all matter is composed of one form or another of the same higher dimensional substances. In other words, to the new species (or intelligences), the universe would appear just as solid as the previous universe appeared to the older form of humans.

Recall that the older, denser, more physical human body way back eons ago was mostly composed of empty space. The new beings are even more rarefied as they exist on a higher vibrational level.

The average human body of the older *Homo Sapiens Sapiens* species was composed of approximately 99.9999999% empty space. However, if our atoms are mostly separated by just empty space, why can't we pass through other physical objects?

We need to re-examine what we mean by empty space. Space is never truly empty. It's actually full of wave functions, invisible quantum fields, and more.

The majority of the mass of an atom is found in the positively charged nucleus that is primarily composed of protons and neutrons that are themselves the manifestation of an even deeper layer, the quarks. Thus, these protons and neutrons are not truly solid.

Strictly speaking, electrons (that have a negative charge) are point sources, therefore they occupy no volume. A true point is infinitely small. However, they do have what we term a wave function that occupies the vast majority of the interior space within an atom.

Because quantum mechanics is more than weird, the volumeless electron wave function thus occupies the majority of internal volume of the atom. In effect, the electrons are "spread out" or "smeared out" in most of the whole of the internal volume of an atom. While protons and neutrons to a similar extent are also "smeared out" they occupy a more defined location within the nucleus.

The electrons flash around the inside of the atom occupying portions of the inner space with their wave functions, thus the atom's internal volume is always taken up; therefore on the outside it appears or seems to be solid.

The consequence of this is that you have never actually touched anything at all—ever. For example, close your finger and thumb together so that they are pressing against each other. Despite your sense of touch telling you otherwise, your fingers will never actually meet. In other words, your fingers will never contact one another, because they are separated by an electromagnetic force that keeps them fractionally apart.

Be that as it may, our sense of touch tells us that our fingers really are touching, but in reality they never do. So what do we actually touch, then?

What we do feel is the sensation of the electromagnetic force of some of your bodily electrons in one finger pushing against the electrons in the other finger.

As previously mentioned, the new humans would "feel" their world as being just as solid as it appeared to their predecessors. Thus, a new human would still have to move aside when meeting another person to avoid a collision, because it would still experience a sense of touch as before.

Bar-Ax-an

The New Lineage

1. The Sky Rider

"Sir, we have a problem."

Number One was seated at his desk with his back to his second-in-command. He was in his late fifties, with his temples now sporting a smattering of gray amongst his still mostly curly black hair. "What is it, Number Two?"

"We've just discovered that there is a large metallic object in orbit around Ixl, sir."

"Is it one of ours?"

She replied, "No, we don't think so sir."

"When did you discover it?"

"It appeared just a couple of days ago sir."

"How could it suddenly appear—just like that?"

"We believe that it employed some form of cloaking device. There is a possibility that the device is now malfunctioning, which is why we've only just seen it. I didn't report it at the time as I decided to order checks on its authenticity first sir."

"Good work Number Two. What did you find?"

"Sir, we believe that this object has been in orbit for possibly millions of years. We've discovered that it is composed of a hard metallic substance that is impervious to our probes."

"Millions of years? That doesn't seem possible! If that's the case, it would predate our entire civilization by a huge margin, wouldn't you say?"

"Indeed sir, that's why I ran a series of checks on it. We also discovered that its orbit is gradually deteriorating, which is why I'm bringing it to your attention now."

Number One swung around in his tan leather bucket chair to face his second-in-command. With a serious expression, he asked, "You mean that it will crash into our planet?"

"Eventually, yes sir, but we calculate that it won't happen for several centuries or more."

"Okay, well that's a relief Number Two, but we still need to determine what it's here for and what form of intel it is gathering—if any. Arrange a meeting of all the heads of state for tomorrow morning on your Pacat. This is urgent."

"Yes sir, will do sir."

Number Two turned and hurriedly departed, her flowing rainbow-pigmented electrostatically charged clothing crackling as she went.

Number One coolly surveyed his glittering domain, much of it composed of a material resembling stainless steel, though in reality it was plasmoid in nature. The miles-high conical buildings shone with a yellow tinge in the evening starlight in the gathering dusk.

He thought gloomily, "This is really bad news. I've come across references to this object before, but I've ignored them due to time constraints. Now that its presence has been formally noted, that will bring attention to the object. That's the last thing we need right now."

He snapped out of his reverie, got up and made his way to his spartanly appointed apartment situated just above his offices. He noted a message on his Pacat informing him that the next day's meeting would be slightly delayed and would now take place at 11:00 am Ixl time. He sighed.

The following morning, Number One sat at his Pacat screen as he waited for the other heads of state to log in.

One by one, the twelve heads of state came online. Number One spoke first once all were present, "Good morning ladies and gentlemen, I hope all of you are sufficiently alert to have noticed a recent development that each one of us needs to be made aware of.

"I have asked you all here because Number Two and her staff have brought to my attention that there is possibly a foreign object in our solar system. Indeed, this thing is orbiting Ixl as we speak."

Number Four quickly asked, "What type of foreign object do you mean sir? Is it an asteroid, a comet or something else?"

"Thank you Number Four. To clarify, it appears to be some type of device that has come from outside our solar system, though that is yet to be confirmed.

"It looks like a type of apparatus that could possibly be collecting information about our civilization or our planet."

Number Seven commented, "What sort of device do you mean? How long has it been collecting this information?"

"Preliminary info shows that it's been orbiting Ixl for possibly several million years. As to what type of intel it is actually gathering, we have no idea so far."

Number Twelve voiced what was already on everyone's minds, "Is it hostile?"

Number One commented, "We simply don't know at this stage Number Twelve. Frankly, if it's been there for several million years, then being hostile is unlikely, otherwise we would all have been obliterated by now."

Number Two promptly responded, "We have gone as far as we can without sending up instruments to determine its composition that might also allow us to discover its purpose in our solar system."

Number One stated matter-of-factly, "We will need to send up a probe to examine this object at close hand. All of us must now take a vote on whether we should act on this information or not. The question is, do we send up a probe to further investigate this object? Please indicate your 'yes' or 'no' decision on your Pacats now."

All but Number Six gave a "yes" vote.

Number One noted Number Six's negative response on his Pacat, so inquired, "Number Six, why did you vote as you did? The majority voted to send up a probe, but you did not. What was behind your reasoning?"

"I feel it may be very dangerous to approach this object closely, and use instruments that attempt to probe its interior sir. We don't know what feathers our actions may ruffle. What if the device is inactive and we inadvertently wake it up?"

"Thank you Number Six, that's a valid point. However, it's a case of damned if we do, and damned if we don't. We have no choice, we have to investigate it to determine what our next move will be. Depending on what we find, we may leave it as it is, or be forced to destroy it. There does not appear to be any middle ground.

"I therefore abide by the majority decision. We will send up a craft to explore the object as soon as we can arrange a package of suitable instruments."

Number One cracked his gavel hard on the tabletop to indicate the discussion was closed.

A suitable craft sent up three days later contained several artificially intelligent tools that could be useful in analyzing the object's interior and that may also assist in understanding the device's purpose.

The spaceship cautiously approached the visitor from afar taking measurements as it drew nearer. Probing the visitor's interior, the craft drew a blank. The interior could not be interrogated by any of its instruments. Therefore it was only possible to discover something about the object from its emanations, but currently none were found.

Once the information gathering stage had been concluded, Number One read through the reports and charts pertaining to the object. It seemed that occasionally there were electromagnetic anomalies that were in the form of short bursts of energy, but no one had previously connected these with the unknown device.

He got on his Pacat to Number Two, "See if you can find a radio telescope that has collated info on that damn thing. We've got virtually nothing on it so far. We need something to go on before I will order its destruction. There may be a radio telescope that still exists, which is situated in the old country of Ukraine. It used to be located in the Yevpatoria region. As far as I recall, it can also transmit so it may be extremely useful in its ability to run tests on the thing. Try that one first."

Number Two responded, "Yes sir. I'll attend to that as soon as we have finished our call."

Number Two contacted the telescope facility, who it turned out were only too happy to help. She then contacted Number One again, once a comprehensive suite of tests had been run on the object.

A Pacat meeting was then hurriedly convened with the telescope's Chief Operator Kirril Orlyk and the twelve sector heads of state.

Once the participants were settled, Number One asked, "Chief Operator Kirril Orlyk, thank you. We are grateful for your help and investigations. Briefly, what have you come up with so far?"

Orlyk replied, "This has been a very unusual case. Initially we passively explored the full radio spectrum to see if the device was emanating anything unusual, but we drew a blank. However, that does not mean it has never done so in the past, only that our findings are inconclusive.

"We then switched to actively probing the device—if we can call it that. We did several scans at various resolutions, but only the highest resolution revealed anything. To give you an example, this resolution is the equivalent of standing about ten feet away from a large wall that has writing about three or four inches high on its surface.

"We found the object is entirely covered in what appears to be a form of hieroglyphs."

Number One was the first to speak following a shocked silence, "...This is incredible! Are you saying that this object is related to the ancient Egyptians?"

"Yes sir, but only partially. In some ways the inscriptions appear to be similar in concept to early forms of script that perhaps fostered the later evolution of what we now refer to as hieroglyphs.

"You might also care to note that we ran some brief samples of the script through a translator, but while there are indeed some correspondences and there is quite a bit of overlap, much of the language is unknown to us. Languages are not our forte."

"Thank you again Chief Operator Kirril Orlyk for your and your staff's contributions. We will be in touch with further questions very soon," Number One briefly commented before closing the communication.

Number Two then spoke up, "Number One sir, can we give these scans to our languages department? They also have a far more powerful computer that could make more sense of these characters."

Number Four broke in, "That seems a good idea to me sir. It seems imperative that we attempt to understand where this object came from and its intentions."

"Okay," announced Number One, "we will have a yes or no vote. The question to all of you is, do we proceed with investigating these inscriptions or not? Please cast your votes now."

There was a 100% yes vote for carrying out further investigations. A month later, the results came in.

2. Multidimensional Entities

After a further week had passed, at another hastily convened Pacat meeting Number One intoned, "We have completed our research for the present, and reached some important conclusions that all of us here must be made aware of.

"First, this object has been in orbit for several thousand years, and not millions as suggested previously, thus it is a fairly recent addition to our solar system. We have studied the so-called glyphs and while we have not been able to interpret some of the characters, we have made sense of much of it in sufficient detail for us to pass this critical information on to you."

Number Six took advantage of a short pause to inquire, "What was the basis for the translation? Was the script similar to any known Ixl-based language?"

"Yes indeed. While there are no current similar scripts, we checked old Terran based databases, and came up with a match. It most closely resembles Akkadian cuneiform writing that comprises roughly 600 to 1,000 characters. In those early times, the symbols were impressed in soft clay with a simple tool, or stamped on very thin sheets of metal to spell words by dividing them up into syllables.

"In other words, two or more symbols may be used to pronounce a word. Thus, the two symbols 'ba-at' would be used to pronounce the word 'bat'. Occasionally, other symbols could also denote complete words as well.

"It also incorporates other graphic symbols that resemble hieroglyphics, which may possibly be a later development. These in fact are what, so far, are presently preventing a complete translation. However, we have managed to read much of the cuneiform script and bypass the rest."

Number Three asked, "And what has the script revealed so far?"

"Essentially we've found that this object was created by beings originating from the binary star system we know as Sirius, which is also known as the Dog Star. As far as we can tell, they are multidimensional beings who have visited us on several occasions in the past."

Number Five spoke up, "What do you mean by multidimensional beings?"

"Apparently they are able to move between several dimensions. To us humans who, as far as we are aware, exist in just three dimensions, it appears as if they are able to simply appear or disappear at will."

Number Five added, "Then how do we fight or combat this species? As I understand it, we have nothing that can detect such beings. How do we defend ourselves?"

Uproar broke out as the ramifications of what had just been uttered sank in.

Number One roared, "Please, please, ladies and gentlemen, order, order!" He banged his gavel several times until the riotous commotion had subsided.

Number Two spoke first, "If this is true, what do we do about it? Should we destroy the object?"

Number One declared, "I've taken advice from my war cabinet and the brainiacs have determined that the best course of action is to just leave it well alone. After all, it has already been here for thousands of years, and has apparently done us no harm.

"If we destroy it, its owners make take exception to that and treat it as an act of war and come looking for us.

"We need to make a decision on the proposed course of action to observe and do nothing for the present. That is the option. Do I have a yes? Please vote for your decision on your Pacats now."

All present affirmed that the present status quo continued to offer the best solution for the time being.

After several years, the object did not attract any further attention, and because it was no longer considered as being newsworthy, it simply faded from view in the collective consciousness of the masses.

Ella

Love is an affinity – a synchronization.

Bar-Ax-an

The prophet Ella described consciousness thus:

Consciousness, she like a fair woman,

The Beloved,

She has many faces.

Sometimes she all sweetness and light,

Other times she sultry and welcoming,

She also dark and has her moods.

Sometimes she get very angry,

So you better run for your life,

She going to kill you if she get a hold of you.

She all of those things and more—all at the same time.

Information

In this second phase several thousand years in Ixl's future, the prophet Ella is born. She has come to do battle with an enemy which has returned to the solar system from the far reaches of space.

On the battlefield she allies with some of the armies of The Highest Impulse who are ranged before her to both her left and right.

However, no distinction can be made here between so-called "right" or "wrong", as all are created by The Highest Impulse. Both terms can be learned from and acted upon. Following the correct evolutionary path for humanity is the sole determining factor.

This momentous battle would determine whether the human experiment would succeed or fail, and whether this new universe—or Day of Brahma—would evolve sufficiently to be ratcheted up into a yet higher dimension in its next iteration, or conversely disappear into oblivion.

Bar-Ax-an

1. The Beginning

Ella grew up as an abandoned ragamuffin child. As she matured, her flowing red hair and freckles soon became her trademark. Most of her family had been exterminated in the brutal wars on the enemy planet Vrakis. Her parents had been killed in a ferocious battle between her own hominid species and the cybernetic AI organisms that appeared crudely human in appearance. Oftentimes, the only way to tell the two species apart was to study their mannerisms and their use of language. The cybernetics' occasional wrong usage of a word or a misplaced phrase were often the only clues that gave the game away.

As a child of the city of Node's slums, Ella had little education, so she was forced to care for herself and her two younger brothers Billy and Grant by living on the streets. Ella badly missed her parents. She alone had to shoulder all responsibility for the welfare of her two siblings.

In the main, they managed to live off scraps or handouts, and consequently Ella had to rely on her wits and develop her inner sensitivities in order for them to survive in their hostile environment. As a matter of course, she soon became able to "read" people's intentions. This helped her small family survive where otherwise quite probably they would not.

It was on a dull misty day that she first met Durne while out shopping for food. She had collected a few credits from begging on the streets, so was out buying something to give to her brothers to eat. It was in a shopping mall that she literally bumped into her future mentor. Durne was a kindly man with a light build and graying hair. In age, he appeared to be around his mid-fifties.

They would often meet in the local park amidst the kids playing ball, lovers out for a walk, or young men out to impress the local girls. Due to the park being small and the populace large, people would often accidentally rub shoulders or bump into one another. This often resulted in conversations being interrupted when other people passed between them. However, it was an accepted way of life. It was what it was.

Durne introduced Ella to concepts that she had not come across before. She'd never even heard of the concepts of good or evil, nor of a supreme being who was the embodiment of consciousness. Her world consisted purely of survival against the odds. As long as she was able to provide a little food for her brothers and herself, she was content.

Eventually, she educated herself in a rudimentary manner, enough to understand that she and her kind embodied a Life Force or Spirit that, once it had been finely honed, was more precious than all the gold on the planet put together.

She understood that collectively they must fight for the right to endure, but at the same time actions must have a basis in truth, and not just mimic what the mass media had force-fed them. The huge media screens situated on almost every street corner were designed to indoctrinate, to keep people in the dark. They were oblivious to the controllers behind the scenes and their motives, who had no intention of educating or enlightening them, just feeding off them like parasites.

She had learned to stand tall and think for herself. Her brutal world had forced her to grow up fast and to uphold what she saw as truth.

While it is true that she had been given a certain form of energy that was palpable, it was only by being part of a group moving forward with the same values as herself that her small band was able to overcome the huge odds stacked against them.

It had been well known for almost as long as the human race existed that groups have a certain energy that is magnified and is greater than simply the combination of their constituent parts. If this were not so, businesses and companies or even nations would never have come into existence. As an analogy, flocks of birds swoop and turn together as if they are one body.

Equally, this form of understanding requires a person to become the focus of attention who is capable of motivating the entire group. It may also embody financial or other rewards; or alternatively offer something much deeper, as is the case of Ella the prophet-to-be, but it always requires some form of guide who is deeply motivated to move the group forward.

And so it was that Durne taught her all that he knew in his little run-down apartment. Ella's heart had become purified of dross not just by absorbing his teachings and methods, but also by actively employing them in the interactions within her seemingly impoverished world. His efforts or principles had to be interpreted in such a way that consciously and unconsciously she would embody love and compassion, which would become her foundation based on Reality.

Her inner sensitivities had also become sharpened to such an extent that she was able to sense the intent and actions of those beings who primarily lived and acted in the higher dimensions. Obviously her five ordinary senses such as sight or hearing were of little use at such levels, but it was possible to infer what these beings were attempting to accomplish even if she could not directly see or hear them.

Thus it was that one day, she was given a message embedded in her environment that could only have come from these beings in the higher dimensions. She received a call to action.

As a poorly educated person with no notion of why she'd been given this task, nor any idea of how she might carry out such a mission, Ella at least understood that somehow she must engage the forces of so-called evil.

While it was occasionally necessary to carry out actions that could be interpreted as "evil" for the betterment of humankind, she understood that under the present conditions, she had to utterly destroy these forces for the universe as a whole to evolutionarily move forward.

There would be no huge armies to help Ella, just her small band of faithful helpers who saw and believed in what had been instilled in her. They would fight to the death to help overcome the forces of darkness that surrounded all. Without words, these people knew on another level that they must employ the power of compassion to successfully override those malevolent forces.

Ella was also given to understand that she must incorporate all her practical knowledge—along with the directions given by the entities from the higher dimensional worlds—to guide her.

However, underneath it all, Ella was deeply afraid. She was not afraid of dying, for that is inevitable for each one of us, but she was afraid that she was not up to the task that she had been given.

It took Ella some considerable time to accept that none of us is perfect and we all make mistakes, but she also understood that it is one's intention that counts. She knew that her intentions were unsullied by human affairs or concerns.

2. The Adversaries

Ella was coming into her prime. Her hair graying at the roots, she still cut a regal figure despite her lowly origins. She'd heard of interdimensional beings before. Durne had mentioned them on many previous occasions as had several of her other associates. Durne had intimated that she may have to meet these entities at some point, and that she might even have some form of adversarial contact with them.

She'd even been informed that many of these beings were definitely not friendly toward humans, and even coldly viewed them as the dregs of the universe whom they could exploit with no qualms.

"Where do these beings come from?" Ella asked Durne on one dark drizzly autumn day.

He replied, "Well, we are not able to know for sure, as we do not have their abilities to slide in and out of different dimensions, but we understand that they originate from the binary star system called Sirius. We believe they come from Sirius A's fifth planet that we refer to as Exit 5."

Ella commented, "We've heard of references to Sirius before, but why that planet's unusual name?"

"That's because we think there are several convolutions in space and time in its immediate vicinity, or more simply put, there is a vortex there that may form some sort of wormhole in space. It is a form of exit from this three-dimensional universe into another reality, hence its name.

"We think that these beings who we have named Archons use this wormhole to travel to other distant destinations.

"However, ancient texts and prophecies also tell us that they have visited us eons ago, so there is a possibility that if they still exist, they may return again at some point."

"Hah, that doesn't seem like a likely prospect to me."

"Don't scoff Ella, as myths and many old tales can often contain more than a kernel of truth. While the originators' experiences were real, they often didn't have the required vocabulary or concepts to convey what they saw or felt, so they framed what they saw in their own contexts."

Ella coolly replied, "Okay, I'm prepared to put my prejudices aside for the minute. So what do we know of these creatures you refer to as Archons?"

"I'm sorry, but I can't tell you more offhand as it is not my specialism, so you'll need to look this up on your Pacat. I'm sure there must be a lot of info out there on the subject."

"Okay, thanks Durne for talking to me, I'll definitely look into it." Ella then made her apologies, and sauntered off to her room. Once settled, she coupled her Pacat up to a large virtual screen, and then spent some time seeking the info she needed.

Eventually, she queried the device, "Myths about Archons."

Instantly a page full of data and links appeared along with a few grainy images.

She sat quietly on the edge of her bed for a couple of minutes as she absorbed the info.

She thought, "Tall... Hooves on their two feet, they stand upright... Scales... A tail, and smelling of sulfur to boot! Ugh!! These images portray them as devils! Surely such beings cannot really exist... This is the stuff of nightmares!"

Frightened, she hastily switched off the display, and tried to put the grotesque images out of her mind.

Ella did not sleep at all well that night. She tossed and turned continually. Her sleep was punctuated with recurring nightmares. She imagined these creatures on their home planet in what can only be described as a vision of hell. The alien landscape was permeated with volcanoes belching dark acrid smoke and ashes with rivers of molten lava under a dull red leaden sky.

She woke with a start in a cold sweat and jerked her body upright. As she came to, she told herself to breathe calmly and settle down—after all it was all just a dream…

However, the nightmare would not go away. She attempted to get back off to sleep. She would close her eyes but would still see these creatures in her mind's eye. Ella decided to visit Durne in the morning to ask him what the dream could mean.

Daylight came as Ella wearily rubbed her sore and itchy eyes. She felt exhausted after her dreadful night, but she knew she must see Durne, and it had to be now. She hastily dressed, and gobbled down her breakfast before messaging him to let him know she would soon be arriving, then set off.

Fifteen minutes later, she stood outside the door to Durne's apartment. She pressed the intercom and announced herself, "Hi Durne, it's me. Sorry, I know it's early, but this is really important. Can I come in?"

After a short pause, a groggy voice replied, "Ella, what the hell do you want at this hour? It's not even seven am for goodness' sake!"

"Sorry Durne, I did message you..."

Durne interrupted, "...I didn't see it yet. It's way too early! What is it you want anyhow?"

"I need to talk about the Archons..."

"Now? Why now? Hmm... I wondered when you'd get around to that. It's sooner than I thought."

"Can I at least come in? It's freezing out here!"

"Okay, you can wait in my dining room while I get dressed. Have you had breakfast yet?"

"Yes, I'm fine thanks."

"I'm famished, so you'll just have to put up with me eating while we talk."

The intercom glowed green to allow Ella to enter. Then the shiny metal door opened with a slight hissing sound. Ella cautiously stepped forward.

"It's the second door on the right," a distant voice announced.

Ella, conscious that she'd interrupted Durne's sleep, tiptoed into the dining room. She'd never been in this room before. Durne had previously always met her in some public place. She had also attended a meeting or two in his living room, but she had no idea of what this part of his apartment looked like on the inside.

She stood in the center of the room, waiting patiently with hands clasped behind her back for Durne to finish showering. In a couple of minutes, a dripping Durne appeared wrapped in a large bath towel.

"Please take a seat. I'll be finished in a minute. Are you sure you won't have something? A hot drink maybe?"

"Oh, okay, I'll have a coffee thanks, but I'll wait for you to finish first."

But Durne had by now already stepped back into his bathroom to complete his morning routine so didn't hear her. A few minutes later, he appeared again but this time fully clothed.

He walked over to the food dispenser and pressed a button. He murmured, "The usual please..." And questioningly, "Two cups of coffee?"

"Yes thanks, coffee is fine for me."

He then turned to ask her, "By the way, I don't remember, how do you like your coffee?"

"Oh, strong, without milk, but with three sugars."

Durne repeated it to the machine, which duly presented him with his cornflakes and two mugs of steaming coffee. He ambled over to the dining table and as he did so, invited Ella to accompany him.

After sitting down and a mouthful or two of coffee, Durne broke the ice and asked Ella directly, "So Ella, you got me out of bed to ask about the Archons. What's the urgency at this hour of the morning?"

Ella cupped her warm mug in her hands, elbows on the table as she began, "Durne, I used my Pacat to look into ancient myths and came across references to the Archons.

"I explored the topic more thoroughly as you said, but I didn't like what I found. Somehow, seeing the images of what they are supposed to look like caused me to have nightmares.

"It is as if the images stirred up some deep racial memory within me, as if there is some truth to all of this. But I can't believe that this can be true, so I came here to get reassurance that this was simply just a bad dream. Did I do the right thing?"

Durne stopped eating, slowly put his spoon down, and then looked at her steadily for a minute. "I tried to fob you off before, pretending that I knew nothing about these creatures, but I see that you went into it a lot deeper than I had anticipated.

"I was going to broach the subject with you at a more appropriate time, but how I might initiate the topic was the difficult issue. In a way, this nightmare of yours has made it much easier for me to introduce the subject."

Ella smiled uneasily as she waited for Durne to continue.

"…Okay, so let's begin then. First off, these beings have been here before, many eons ago. They come from a planet named Exit 5 that orbits one of the stars in the binary star system Sirius. They have discovered a method of traveling through space by using a wormhole to get to distant planets.

"They are a narcissistic warlike race that has little or no emotion. They will use anything to their advantage—if they can. And because they are technologically advanced, that includes utilizing anything and everything on the entire planet, including its livestock for their own purposes."

"Do you mean that they treat the indigenous intelligent native species like livestock? Surely you can't be serious?"

"I'm afraid that I am indeed quite serious. Essentially they will genetically manipulate the existing dominant species on any planet they come across into lifeforms they can exploit.

"For example, they will create worker races that have minimal intelligence who can only understand simple directions—or they will farm other species as a food source. Yet again, for instance, they will create other beings whose minds are suitably modified for carrying out, erm, more lowly menial tasks."

"I can't believe that! Surely this is a joke? You must be pulling my leg!"

Durne sighed, and then slowly answered, "I wish I really was just pulling your leg Ella, but I'm not. This is real, this is all true."

Ella sat passively for a minute taking it all in, then slowly sipped her by now lukewarm coffee.

She thought for a few more seconds then murmured, "So how did these creatures depart? I mean, what caused them to leave this planet, or did they simply die out?"

"Well, they didn't just die out. We know that for sure, but it seems that there was some sort of disagreement between different factions. A war ensued but we don't know if it was just a war over ownership of this planet, minerals, or whether the dispute was more expansive to cover other worlds as well.

"The upshot was that they depleted many valuable resources on this planet and took most of the remaining materials when they left, but we have heard nothing since."

Ella commented, "So if they didn't die out or exterminate themselves, presumably they must've gone home, so might return at some point?"

"I'm afraid that that's about right. There is some talk that this may indeed happen—and soon."

"I need to think about this and its ramifications. Frankly, I don't like the way this topic is going at all.

"Please don't get me wrong, it isn't you, it's just that this is a deeply disturbing subject. Can we leave it like that for now?"

"Sure, no problem. I understand that this topic must be deeply disturbing for you. We can resume when you are ready."

Ella shook Durne's hand, smiled, said her goodbyes and then set off to walk to her own home.

She hoped the fresh morning air would clear her head.

They Come

1. The Wormhole

Several years passed following that fateful conversation. In fact, Ella had almost completely forgotten that it ever happened. Now and again the subject would surface in her thoughts, but she suppressed them immediately as mere speculation, so did not give the notion any more attention. Besides, the prospect of anything coming from such a distant star seemed improbably remote.

Then one day while she was out panhandling in the streets, an emergency broadcast aired with accompanying video on all media channels that was also displayed on the huge video panels in the street:

> "We interrupt this broadcast. A large wormhole has opened near Jupiter in our solar system. We believe this is a portal from another dimension. Several fireballs have been seen exiting the perturbation, and appear to be under intelligent control. We are closely monitoring the situation, and will keep you informed of any further developments."

The screen faded, and normal programming was resumed. Ella sighed and turned away from the trashy show that replaced the broadcast. However, this episode visibly shook her up and reminded her of that fateful discussion with Durn just a few years ago. Her recall had a curious effect on her, causing her legs to shake. She needed to sit down to steady herself and think. She relaxed on a nearby old rickety public bench to regain her composure.

However, Ella was hungry, and desperate to find food, so she soon had to pull herself together and get on her still wobbly feet. She decided to continue panhandling, but this time she would try her luck in the local shopping mall. She had been thrown out the last time, so she was careful to avoid the guards.

At the back of her mind she also remembered to keep her attention on the huge media panels, which much of the time displayed mindless adverts designed to stimulate the masses' thirst for new products and thus increase profits for the controllers behind the scenes. Nevertheless, this time she was apprehensive about those so-called fireballs. She sensed something was wrong. Very wrong indeed.

However, nothing much happened that day. She had successfully avoided the shopping mall guards and managed to accumulate quite a few credits, certainly enough to feed her two brothers and herself for a few more days. However, she never knew what the next day would bring.

A week later, Ella was out once again begging for credits. Once again a nearby media panel sprang into life displaying an unsettling message in gaudy text:

> "Alert! We have now determined that the fireballs are now on course for Ixl! It appears that these objects seem to be under intelligent control. Astronomers have noted that they slowed perceptibly as they flew past the orbit of Mars. We will keep you informed of further developments."

Another week passed, and then the Archons arrived.

2. Disturbing Proof

The fireballs had altered course to fall into orbit around Ixl (the current name for Terra). Despite a flurry of communication attempts originating from Ixl, there was no response, so to all intents and purposes it appeared that nothing was happening.

Then a man out walking his dog on the Borborema Plateau in Brasil came across a terrifying being that killed his pet. He barely escaped with his life as he fled behind an escarpment. After calming down somewhat, he informed the local police, but was scoffed at as his seemingly mad ramblings did not convey anything anyone could understand.

Then it happened again. This time, it was in Lahore, Pakistan. A couple arm-in-arm came around the side of Lahore Fort to face what they could only refer to as the devil. Screaming, they turned and ran as fast as they could. On this occasion both of them escaped. Two other witnesses who were there at the same time helped to convince the authorities that this was not just some acid trip.

At a loss what to do, the couple went to see the Governor Ali Barbar at his home to report the news. They were shown into a stately waiting room while the Governor assembled his aides so everyone could hear the couple's story.

The Governor in his office sighed, and stood up from behind his mahogany desk. He wryly thought out loud, "Another damn couple trying to make some money with a cock and bull story to scare the shit out of the masses."

Still, he had the decorum to hear them out. It was his duty to protect the population, even if the story was unlikely.

He entered the room as the couple humbly rose to their feet, who then bowed, then both of them clasped their hands together in greeting.

"Sit, please..." the Governor indicated with a flourish of his hands.

After the couple, who were now holding hands, had settled down, the Governor inquired gruffly, "What is it you saw? My aides tell me that it was some sort of scaly devil in appearance."

"Yes sir," the woman started, "it was indeed reddish brown and scaly. It was huge, standing about 7-8 feet tall. It had a pointed tail and cloven hooves like a cow. It had hands like ours, but it had sharp nails and fingers that were much larger than our own. I must also tell you that it smelled badly."

"Of what?"

"I think it was sulfur, but I can't be sure as I don't know what sulfur smells like," the man interjected.

The Governor turned his back, trying to suppress a chuckle as he attempted to envisage such a beast.

"Don't you believe us sir?" the woman chimed in again. "We are humble farmers and we are not prone to drinking or exaggeration. We have babies at home, so we were out for some fresh air as a couple to just be with one another, to get some peace..."

"Yes, yes, I know all that," Barbar snapped. "The issue is not you; it is that we also had reports from Brasil that someone else saw one of these beasts. Apparently it killed a man's dog. The dog's injuries were unlike anything we have ever seen before. They looked like the animal had been clawed to death."

He continued somberly, "I want to show you some images on my Pacat. The man in Brasil has hand-drawn the creature for us so it's rather crude, but it conveys the information we need. I want you to confirm that it is the same sort of a beast as the one you both saw here."

"Of course," the man replied.

The Governor first used his Pacat to create a virtual screen in front of his guests. He then displayed several images. Some alternatives had also been drawn to confuse viewers in an effort to catch them out if they were exaggerating, or being economical with the truth. The woman in her excitement shrieked as she pointed excitedly, "That's it! That's the one! We saw one just like that!"

The Governor scowled as he slowly closed down his Pacat. He was now beginning to understand the seriousness of the situation. He was damn sure that those fireballs had something to do with this, but he needed more information to confirm his suspicions. It was not long in coming.

Compromise

1. We Come in Peace

A fleet of huge black ugly box-shaped craft that sported several external appendages slipped noiselessly over many of the major cities of Ixl including Washington, London, Beijing, Paris, Madrid, Tokyo, Canberra, New Delhi, Lahore, and many more. Each of the spacecraft took up a station above the respective major governmental offices.

Soon after their appearance, which had been clearly visible to all, populations began to riot. Police and the military were required to use major force to disperse the unruly crowds, and the authorities soon had to introduce curfews. All of humanity was metaphorically in chains for the first time in recorded history— but not from the arrival of the visitors, but from those self-inflicted and violent controls that had been placed on the population by their own forces.

The situation continued for eight uproarious days. Then, small craft that resembled glistening transparent soap bubbles began to emerge out of the box-shaped craft. They paused before slowly floating down to land on the front lawns of the various government offices.

The world watched in awe while the entire scene was televised. In astonishment, the populace collectively wondered what would happen next. After about an hour, an opening dissolved in the side of each craft in synchrony with every other craft situated around the globe. Consequently some portals appeared during daylight hours, while others opened in the dead of night, dependent on location. Then a few minutes later, beings matching the description given by the Lahore couple emerged, accompanied by a pungent odor.

It appears now that these creatures either used some sort of translation device, or had learned the local language pertaining to each location, so they could converse with the indigenous population.

Roughly translated, their collective voiced message began like this:

> "We come in peace. We desire to see the leader of your country or sector to discuss our arrival, and what this will entail for both of our populations."

There was no human response for some time. Many heads of state as a precautionary measure had decided to not directly appear face to face with the new arrivals, and instead ordered up the military, who soon appeared in strength.

A being, presumably their commander, spoke again through his translator:

> "This will not do. We have no other option but to neutralize all your weapons. We will not release them until we speak directly with all the heads of state from each country or sector. You have two Ixlan hours to fulfill this obligation, or there will be severe consequences."

Ella, standing in the street watching a nearby media screen, stood there frozen to the spot for a couple of minutes. She wryly thought, "Now you have shown your true colors! Now we know that this is not peace for everyone at all, this is a seizure, a land grab—and bring about a capitulation of the human race!"

Later, while she sat thinking on her park bench, munching half a sandwich, a huge bright airburst exploded overhead. She realized that somehow, someone had managed to trigger an explosion on a military satellite high in orbit. She wondered how many casualties there might be and if any of the visitors' craft had also been destroyed.

Ella soon discovered the terrible truth. The Archons by this time had taken over the huge media screens and displayed the dreadful tragedy. A World Federation military satellite had attempted to ram one of the Archons' spaceships. Both the satellite and a large Archon mothership had been destroyed in the huge blast.

The Archon creatures disappeared, and their box-like craft took off to return to their motherships. All went quiet for a couple of days, then a single bubble craft appeared above the World Federation building situated on an artificial island in the Atlantic. Slowly it descended to land on the imitation grass on the front lawn.

As before, a further hour passed until the door was opened. A single Archon appeared. He/she/it somehow knew that a general meeting was currently in progress in which the world's delegates were discussing a firm response to the earlier satellite destruction.

The Archon simply announced:

> "I call upon Jean Paul Ferrer to come forth now to discuss the terms of a joint leadership."

The Archon had called for Jean Paul Ferrer, who was the current Federation leader, to discuss what would almost certainly be the forced terms of a joint leadership. Jean Paul Ferrer, in his early sixties, was a slightly overweight man with graying hair and pattern baldness.

After a few minutes, Jean Paul appeared from the front of the building, his forehead glistening with beads of sweat. He cowered and clutched his hands together in a sign of deference to the Archon who stood over him by at least a couple of feet.

The Archon began:

> "I repeat, we come in peace. Our mission here is to collect raw materials for our own use that will for the most part be extracted from seawater. We would be honored to offer you 50% of the materials we obtain for your own use, without terms of any other kind."

Jean Paul muttered, "I don't have that authority. We are all sovereign states with our own decision-making processes..."

The Archon breathed:

> "There will be no more states or sectors making their own decisions. All human authority will now exist solely within the walls I see before me.
>
> "Collectively you now have the chance to talk amongst yourselves for two more Ixlan hours, and then if there is still no response, the decision will be made for you. There will be no exceptions or delays allowed."

A meeting was thus hurriedly convened, and a shortlist was drawn up of suitable human candidates who would accept responsibility on behalf of all humanity. It was then handed to the Archon.

> "Good, I see that you have worked together at last to come up with a shortlist of suitable candidates. Now we must set up a further body that is headed by our own Representative who will be in overall control."

"B... b... but that's a dictatorship..." Jean Paul stuttered.

> "Call it what you will, but that is the new situation. We will be in control from this point forward."

The Archon turned, then smartly stepped back inside his craft, and then a few minutes later it simply disappeared into thin air.

The uneasy situation with the Archons in command prevailed for two years. There were now continual skirmishes between the opposing belligerents.

Resistance groups were set up, but on each occasion the Archons were able to locate their secret strongholds and thus they were soon utterly eliminated.

It was to be the rout of humankind.

2. The Kozyrev Device

Luckily, Ella and her two younger brothers Billy and Grant had managed to find shelter in some large natural caverns. The other humans were dispersed in small groups over a large area to avoid all members being captured at the same time.

The humans kept out of sight while they drew up plans for exterminating the Archons. They set up bases in areas where the Archons were spread most thinly such as in the Amazonian jungle, or on the Siberian steppes. Humankind understood that they didn't have the needed power to use physical means to defeat the Archons; they would have to use some alternate form of energy drawn from a different dimension.

Relations between the Archons and humans had deteriorated to such an extent that it was now obvious that open warfare was in the offing.

Thus Durne helped Ella and her colleagues design and build a type of accumulator that could store higher dimensional energy recovered from the so-called "ground state" that is commonly referred to as zero-point energy.

They primarily built and operated two devices. The first, a Kozyrev device, resembled a vertical hollow tubular apparatus about four feet in diameter and about eight feet in height that had mirror-finished inner walls. A door in the side opened to a small seat situated inside.

When a person entered a certain state of mind while quietly seated in the device, it was possible for the "viewer" to see some scenes from the past or alternatively the future to determine probabilities or possible outcomes.

The other device, the accumulator itself, was a power storage device constructed according to certain geometrical principles unknown to the Archons, who simply gave permission for Ella and her crew to construct what they saw as just a weird octagon-shaped building.

When the Archons asked what the "contraption" was for, Ella simply informed them that it was "a place of worship". The Archons laughed at such primitive folly.

Battle Stations

1. Preliminaries

Ella had become battle hardened through taking part in quite a few minor skirmishes. Those lesser clashes along the way had brought her to the standard of fitness she required to succeed in this new endeavor. In the meantime, her band of helpers had also gained much practical fighting experience and had been fine-tuned to form successful battle battalions.

Soon everything was ready for the final assault on the Archons. It was now or never. This opportunity might never come again. It was impossible to assemble such forces out in the open, so in order to fool the Archons, it was necessary to form very small groups. Essentially, they also wanted to appear to be unarmed. They intended to rely on the accumulator to provide them with the capability and strength needed to annihilate the Archons. The device was located at some distance from the battlefield, so relied on a hand-held receiver to activate it.

The device collected and stored energy from the lowest energy level (known as zero-point energy) that pervades everything through a process known as entanglement or the coupling of matter to other matter that was often located at a considerable distance.

It could also accurately be said that the small groups gathered here were simply employed to draw attention away from the accumulator they had brought with them.

What came to be known as the final battle was to be located on a vast plain strewn with the ruins and twisted broken metal of a metropolis long gone.

Ella's small force was dwarfed by the opposition. What kept them all motivated was the belief that they were fighting for a superior cause of which Ella was the embodiment.

The scruffy but battle-hardened band stood on the battlefield, facing their enemies who outnumbered them more than one hundred to one. Ella and her helpers understood that this conflict was to determine the ultimate fate of the human race.

Though vastly outnumbered, her small contingent never flinched. Even if they were all killed, they understood that their actions would influence their world, vastly changing its direction for all time.

Falling to her knees, filthy and bedraggled, Ella recalled the ancient scrolls that had been secreted away, which recounted the exploits of Lutor and his family. Though she could comprehend that truth will always win out in the end, there were still some things she did not understand.

The first question that sprang to her mind was to inquire how those tatty scrolls that Bar-Ax-An had discovered so long ago managed to survive all those eons unscathed? How also did they traverse the dimensions in which they previously existed?

However, she recalled that though the universe would soon be on a higher turn of the spiral in the next Day of Brahma, it still contained all that had gone before, hence traces of what had existed previously would continue to subsist on some level.

She also understood that other similar scrolls from different eras had also miraculously survived. Be that as it may, she didn't want to think too hard about the issue on the battlefield, so simply put it down to providence. Other vastly more important issues must take precedence.

Ella's second query needed The Highest Impulse to directly answer her most earnest supplication, "Oh Eternal One, I ask you as your servant, how it is that Lutor managed to overcome the forces of Darkness in his own era that I similarly face?"

Quick as a flash, the answer crystallized in her consciousness, almost feeling like a memory from within her own being that had lain unbidden, embedded in her muscles themselves.

Her inner voice simply told her, "It is not what you believe, it is what you do, and the use of those powers of ultimate Truth invested in you that I have entrusted to you.

"The forces of so-called evil and good are equal but for one thing. It does not matter whether you class it as good or bad. Names are of no importance, for they are only labels. What counts is which side of the divide to which you and your kind belong that will decide the outcome."

2. The Battle

Ella unsteadily got onto her bleeding and battered legs, her army fatigues tattered into rags. She coolly surveyed the ravaged battlefield that was to decide the future for all Times to come. She took in the smoking debris, and the twisted broken machinery that littered the ground from one horizon to the next, and seemingly on into infinity.

Then above all the destruction, Ella felt the warmth of the golden sun and saw the clear blue sky with the puffy white clouds scudding by. She realized then that despite all the hardships and pain, she had received her message and had already won. All that remained now was to go through the motions and complete the final act.

She understood that the unknowable Oneness of The Highest Impulse had created the Life Force as an extension of Itself, and therefore would always succeed so long as He/She/It willed it. Humanity and other sentient species may occasionally come close to extinction, but the Life Force if necessary would never fail to create anew.

She broke her reverie as she tightly clutched the silver rod-shaped accumulator receiver that would draw energy from the accumulator itself and focus the force onto her enemy. The energy was conscious in its own right, and could only be focused or directed by an entity that was considered sufficiently endowed with the appropriate unsullied characteristics.

To the left stood the Archons—the so-called evil ones and their cohorts. Ella surveyed their AI robots and the Archons' electromechanical devices, which employed rigid inflexible reasoning derived from sophisticated binary computing devices that in years gone by had rained desperation and destruction over all. She understood that their rigid thinking patterns with their lack of flexible thinking would eventually result in their downfall.

To the right stood an almost invisibly tiny Ella with only her small army based around Truth to protect and support her. Ella's troops had little or no equipment compared to their opposition, but all were well trained, and could keep a level head in the heat of the battle. They would fight mercilessly to the end knowing Truth was on their side. Their cause would see to that.

Ella flinched as she realized that it was now time. She summoned all her energy, and then pounded her hands in the air over her head towards the heavens. Next, she drew her hands down to point her receiver at the enemy, and screamed with all her might, "Be no more, Archons, Princes of Darkness! For we are given the power of Truth, and we will defeat Thee!"

Ella knew that this was the last utterance she and her band would ever make, but also knew that their and her own sacrifice were necessary for the universe to continue evolving into the next iteration, the coming Night and Day of Brahma.

After seemingly just a microsecond, a band of piercingly white-hot plasma erupted from her silver controller, dancing from every Archon and onto their equipment as they entered oblivion.

Then in another similar timescale, once the destruction was complete on Ixl, the blinding plasma fire leapt into the heavens to obliterate the entire Archon fleet. The universe then suddenly but noiselessly became serene, as if even the heavens themselves understood that it was all over.

And so, as if by command, perhaps just a second or so later, the universe folded inwards as if it had just been sucked into the vortex of an enormous black hole, and disappeared back into the mind of The Highest Impulse—never for this iteration to be seen again.

To an outsider watching this event, it would appear as if an unknown force of some kind had initiated this terrible calamity. Only those who were aware of the inner workings of The Highest Impulse would be able to comprehend what had just happened.

It was Ella and her small band's sacrifice that had triggered the collapse of the universe—the old Day of Brahma, which enabled Brahma himself/herself/itself to start anew once again—for one and for all in the name of the evolution of humanity...

The Hierarchy in Dreamtime

What is improbable becomes probable.

What is probable becomes commonplace.

What is commonplace transforms into the improbable,

In the next iteration.

Ella

1. Gathering Information

The universe in the form of matter as found in the three plus one dimensions with which we are already familiar was held in abeyance for many eons while the Hidden Hierarchy debated its future. The Hierarchy visualized what was to come in the new Day of Brahma while they resided within what came to be known as The Dreamtime, which was a type of "testing ground" for differing potentialities. It was a place of virtual possibilities only.

Many scenarios would still have to be thoroughly worked out, and then tested before any one of them could be implemented. At present, these alternative universes were only virtual conceptions that may or may not result in actuality.

Some within the Hierarchy argued that the experiment known as humanity had failed, and thus must be dissolved to start again with the lessons learned that would then be actuated within another space/time continuum.

To debate this issue, these Supreme Intelligences came together using a form of telepathy to initially determine the nature of space and time itself in its present form as applied to the previous three plus one dimensions of the last universe. Many of the so-called constants or laws of the universe had changed since that last iteration, or Day of Brahma, so would need to be looked at anew.

In order to manipulate space and time, it was necessary to fully understand its workings in its last incarnation. The fact was that the majority of the Hierarchy were unfamiliar with its current workings, so needed a refresher course to bring them up to speed.

Once this had been accomplished, it was then possible to manipulate data to create other theoretical scenarios. Time could now, for example, be manipulated so that it may no longer exist as a fluid concept flowing ceaselessly along a timeline from the past to the future.

For instance, rather than flowing continuously, time could take the form of discrete quanta (or chunks) that are then assembled within consciousness to seemingly create motion, similar to how a movie is created from stills that are run one after another into seemingly seamless movement.

With this in mind, the collectivity known as the Hierarchy had assembled within this dimension of the Dreamtime to argue the fate of humanity, and thus the fate of Creation itself.

It must be stated here that humankind has been, and still is, pressured to evolve at very close to its capacity to cope, but humanity must achieve its evolutionary goals, as other aspects (pieces of the puzzle) are also waiting to evolve, but are being held back by humanity's slow and often patchy progress.

Telepathically the Hierarchy (or more specifically the Supreme Council) called on humanity to explain its progress—or lack of it. Each of its prophets would be called in turn to a dais to defend his or her actions, and to share the outcome of their work.

The Supreme Entity now spoke on behalf of the entire Council, "We will now call on our prophets to explain themselves and their actions. We shall call them in the order in which they entered conventional three plus one-dimensional space and time.

"We first call on Lutor Levinson. Please take your place at the dais."

Lutor stood up, and then went over to the podium. The Council waited for him to settle, and then proceeded.

"Please explain your actions and their outcome Lutor."

He began, "The era in which I lived was a time of substantial change. I had to deal with the birth of two new species of humans, of which I was one. My work was aimed at coercing *Homo Sapiens Novus*, who were the successors to *Homo Sapiens Sapiens*, to follow the correct evolutionary path.

"As you know, my own lineage comes from *Homo Sapiens Provectus*, which evolutionarily speaking is a further step up the ladder of human development."

"Yes, yes Lutor, we are well aware of that, because as you will know, we instigated most of that design ourselves. Now, tell us why you carried out the actions that you did, and why."

Lutor cleared his throat, and carried on, "My position was that I'd been called to serve in the name of The Highest Impulse by Gabriel. He appeared to me on several occasions and commanded me to fulfill the role that had been set out for me. If you like, I was called to this task.

"However, I was downright terrified of my calling, and initially tried to deny it. Then, when I did eventually start on my allotted task, I found that degeneration and corruption were the order of the day. In other words, depravity was endemic in the humans' culture. This resulted in my being forced to divert from my original plans in order to first of all overcome these obstacles."

"And what were those original plans?"

"My original concept was to instruct suitable people who were called upon to help humanity by utilizing peaceable means. I endeavored to create a conducive atmosphere in which people could mature and grow in understanding."

"But did you not understand that real knowledge only comes from the Teaching with direct contact from suitable experiences that can only be found in the 'real' world?"

"At the time, no, I did not understand that. I was inexperienced, full of big ideas, but did not have the knowledge or understanding to implement them successfully. I also failed to understand how deep the conditioning of the masses went. Essentially, their conditioning was so profound that they were unable en masse to rise to the level required to make substantial progress.

"I therefore was forced to pass the baton on to my daughter Bodekka. She took my place after I was killed in an explosion."

"So why, then, should we not recommend the human race for destruction?"

"Because they try. They have curiosity. Something embedded in them pushes them to stand up and try again. If they are knocked down, then despite all the odds, they will stand up, and try again.

"Maybe they will not succeed immediately, but they will try again, and eventually they will be successful. It is something in their nature that always pushes them to move forward. Evolutionarily, despite their many setbacks, it seems to be a part of the human spirit."

"I see. Thank you Lutor for your contribution. It was most enlightening. Please take your seat and wait while we debate the matter further."

A short while later, the Supreme Council resumed, "We have reached a conclusion that will be considered once we have heard from all the remaining prophets.

"We now call upon Bodekka, Lutor Levinson's daughter, for her own version of events leading up to and following Lutor's death."

Bodekka rose from her seat to take the podium. With her feisty character, she had brought further drastic changes to humanity. She had expanded on her father's work to now encompass the entire solar system.

She coughed slightly to draw her listeners' attention, and then began, "As you will know, I first discovered that I came from my father's lineage after taking a DNA test that conclusively showed that I was his biological daughter. My father Lutor had sent me a letter asking me to do so at the first opportunity following his death.

"At that time, I was a single mom looking after my fraternal twins Boas and Qila. As a librarian, my wages were, to say the least, meager, so I had difficulties making ends meet. While that was not really a part of my future activities, it sets the stage for what happened next.

"I could think of no way out of my situation—except to meet Queen Ariadne and ask for help. Unfortunately, she did not receive me or my findings at all well. But something in her humanity took pity on me, so she relented and opened her heart to the kids and myself. She then took us to her base on Saturn's moon Tethys."

"And what happened next?"

"Unfortunately, Queen Ariadne was not at all convinced by my story, so she had her own DNA tests carried out on us that eventually confirmed what I had been saying all along.

"She also had several advisors who could accurately foretell the future. They advised Queen Ariadne that I would follow in my father's footsteps, and therefore she was to help me in every way that she could.

"As a result of this, I then undertook extensive military training, and even commanded a starship for a short time before it was destroyed in a brutal skirmish in which I only just got away with my life."

"Bodekka, stick to the point. Of what relevance is this to our present line of questioning?"

"Sirs, it is very relevant because this experience in particular shocked me into taking stock of my situation, and determined me to pursue other avenues. Up till that point, I had become totally engrossed in my own military career.

"Some may say that I was being way too selfish. I had forgotten my *raison d'être*, my very reason for living. Frankly, I had also neglected my kids for some time, so I needed that wake-up call to get my values back in line.

"Once I had settled down and gained more experience of life, I went on to promote my father's teachings throughout the Sol solar system. I also brought my children up using my father's methods; they then followed in my footsteps. Eventually they were able to take his teachings to a far wider audience than I ever could."

"Thank you Bodekka. We are grateful for your information, which is noted and recorded. Now please take your seat while we deliberate."

Bodekka shuffled back to her seat.

Again, the Supreme Council debated for a short time before announcing, "We now call upon Boas and Qila."

The fraternal twins took the podium together. Boas was dressed in a jet-black three-piece tuxedo suit, while Qila wore a flowing all white lightweight chiffon dress.

"In your own words, please give us your contribution to these matters. To reiterate so you do not go too far off topic, why should we not destroy the human race and start over with other more cooperative and flexible sentient beings?"

Qila opened, "Thank you so much for inviting us. If it's okay with you, we will speak alternately to answer your questions."

"That sounds just fine Qila. Both of you have our permission to proceed."

Boas started, "As you will recall, we are Bodekka's fraternal twins. She brought us up with the same values that our grandfather cared so much about. He was always on the side of justice and truth. He cared deeply about humanity, and the direction it was headed.

"He saw that humankind was on the decline and needed assistance. Our family as you know is oriented toward helping humanity forward on its evolutionary path."

It was now Qila's turn. "Our mother Bodekka through her own trials and tribulations brought our grandfather Lutor's teachings to the entire solar system. If you will, our grandfather's work was a civilizing factor in human development…"

Boas broke in, "However, as we grew up, humankind was also developing evolutionarily speaking, and now had the technology to reach out to the nearer stars, but not the culture or the refinements that go with it."

Qila resumed next, "Many of these so-called explorers in other star systems were uncivilized both in thinking, and in their living conditions. A better way of looking at it is to say that they were adventurers looking for a better life.

"We termed these people 'rednecks'. Having said that, there were still quite a number of people that understood our mission and wanted to help move humanity forward."

Boas continued, "We often met and then left these more advanced people behind to act as our representatives who would care for their unruly charges. Our aim was to visit them occasionally to check on satisfactory evolutionary progress. The opposite scenario could possibly have held true as well."

Qila finished by adding, "We found that humankind had regressed in many locations, so our aim was to halt any further deterioration, and we maybe even hoped to improve their lot.

"Because of this regressive trait, our task became much harder than originally planned, and thus progress was extremely slow. But I think we can say that we made a difference in the end. Essentially, we doggedly kept to the evolutionary plan for humankind."

"And this was?"

Boas spoke up once more, "To help the universe as a consciousness in its own right to develop and understand Itself. It is, and will remain so over many more eons, essentially a small child, though of course a child infinitely more intelligent than humans could ever hope to be."

Lastly, Qila said, "This intelligence is one in itself, and is as a consequence a oneness—a whole if you will—but because it is an entirety and is a oneness, it cannot visualize itself.

"To give you an example, if a person could not see him, or herself, it would have no way of visualizing itself, or understanding its own nature. It would need a mirror to do that. It is a part of our self-awareness. Animal experiments with mirrors show that most of the higher animals recognize that what they see in a mirror is themselves, and is not just another of their own species.

"Humanity embedded in this universe has this very function for The One. We reflect our nature, our humanity, in the mirror of this universe to inform The Highest Impulse of Itself."

The Supreme Being now spoke to conclude the matter, "I see. Thank you for explaining your own contributions Boas and Qila, and that of your mother Bodekka, and also that of your grandfather Lutor.

"We are eternally grateful to all of you for your service to humanity and the greater good. We do understand that this calling wasn't easy on any of you, but in the context of the evolution of the human race, your roles are of inestimable importance."

Next it was to be the turn of Bar-Ax-an. Though he/she/it was considered to be a learned being, he was not a prophet, but gained a place here due to his standing. He was what many consider to be an AI Intelligence, who oversaw the end of the present universe and The Reversal. However, he was ruled out of the present hearing, because he was not a biological entity.

Instead the Supreme Entity continued by interviewing Ella, "Ella, please come forward and take your place at the dais to explain your actions".

Ella stepped up to the dais to begin summarizing her contribution. She was the last of the prophets who instigated the collapse of the space/time continuum into a gigantic vortex that surrounded a black hole, which instituted the next Night of Brahma.

She nervously cleared her throat, then began, "Ahem, hello, I'm Ella. My duties were not a calling like the others here, but my position was foisted on me by adverse circumstances.

"I could understand that everything was not right in my world, so I started seeking answers. I was lucky to meet someone named Durne who in effect became my guide and mentor. He helped me considerably..."

The Supreme Entity, aware that Ella was having difficulty speaking because she was choking up, muttered slowly, "Yes, yes, please go on. We are all well aware of the role of Durne and the others..."

"Sorry, I was just giving some background info, that's all..."

Ella composed herself, and then started again, "I was educated in the University of Life. I was an urchin living on the street with my two younger brothers Billy and Grant. Somehow, I had to provide for the three of us, so I resorted to begging.

"This background combined with advice from Durne formed a sort of backbone that provided me with an overarching understanding as well as knowledge of how to live my own life. I therefore purified myself of the dross that surrounds us all, but has to be overcome if we as individuals—let alone as a community—are to grow and evolve.

"Fortuitously—or perhaps not—I had learned enough by the time the Archons arrived to understand what needed to be done, as well as now having the mental resilience to take my place as the leader of a small group of rebels who believed in me, and in what I was attempting to do.

"Using the skills I had learned, and my natural intelligence, I was able to defeat the Archons in battle using an accumulator that collected energy from the ground state.

"The consequences of winning the battle were that the time had come for the Universe to revoke Itself. My colleagues, as indeed we all were, were 'dissolved' back into their constituent parts."

The Supreme Entity then asked, "These so-called colleagues of yours. Did they understand what was going to happen to them beforehand?"

"Yes indeed. My colleagues, or helpers if you prefer, understood the finality of what was about to occur. All of them, down to a man or woman, realized that they would be martyred but at the same time understood that we had reached the end of the road. There was no turning back.

"That was the point at which the Highest Impulse sucked the universe into the next Night of Brahma in which we are now situated."

"Thank you Ella, you have accomplished your allotted tasks admirably. I'm sure your talents will be recognized for what they are. However, to reiterate, the Council must find if there has been sufficient cause to prevent the extermination of the human race.

"We must determine if enough effort has been applied by this prophetic line to stop the total dissolution of humanity, and start over.

"We now adjourn this hearing."

The Supreme Entity banged his gavel, and that was that.

2. The Vote

Prophets and guides from other lines of transmission such as Adam's prophetic lineage also held similar Courts to explain their actions. The various Councils would then jointly come together before the Supreme Entity, who is to be the final arbiter.

In Dreamtime the Supreme Council eventually came to a decision. After hearing the evidence provided by Lutor's line of prophets along with evidence from the other Courts, after much deliberation the Council known as the Four Masters held a vote.

It was decided by three votes to one that humanity should continue to evolve in the next iteration of the universe known as the next Day of Brahma, but with some much needed and drastic changes.

The Supreme Entity considered his words carefully, then announced, "I have heard the evidence of my prophets. While it has been a difficult decision, because we have wavered between various outcomes many times, I am now sure that our present decision is the correct one.

"There have been many caveats; however, I have decided that the experiment known as humanity will be allowed to continue in the next iteration of the universe.

"Therefore, before the next universe is planned and constructed, I will need to turn to the Designers, who will carry out extensive updates to the new universe before it is finally brought into existence.

"In particular, I will need to alter the basic laws (rules or patterns) of the universe to accommodate the increase in humanity's intelligence and general shrewdness. In other words, to give the newer species more breathing space to expand and grow.

"I therefore ask the Four Masters to submit these changes for review, and when appropriate, implement them in the design of the new universe."

The Supreme Entity peered expectantly for a minute over his half-glasses at the four seated entities with their upturned faces.

"Do I have a yes?"

In unison the Four Masters replied, "We agree."

Then having received an affirmative reply, the Supreme Entity banged again with his gavel and the deliberations were therefore concluded.

Section Three

The Last Ones

The Universe Begins Again

1. Vran

Information

I am Vran the first prophet at the beginning of the new Day of Brahma. As the first prophet that sprang from a new lineage in the renewed universe, I began anew at the outset of a further spiral of existence, which now took place on a higher dimension or plane.

But first, a short description of progress so far:

It took several billion years for the next iteration of the universe to be designed, constructed, and thoroughly tested during the next Night of Brahma. Progress was carefully concealed within the higher dimensions while the plans were verified, assessed, and any small errors corrected, then finalized to produce the next Day of Brahma. Recall that Brahma is said to live for 100 years (with one year of Brahma equal to 311.04 trillion Terran years) for a total of 8.64 billion years for the combined Day and Night of Brahma.

At last, it and the patterns of the future creatures it would eventually contain were ready. The Four Masters recognized that there would be many teething troubles, and no doubt there would also be a few further defects to be ironed out over time. However, the basic laws of the new universe were in place and operating well.

Nevertheless, small "glitches" may still crop up. For example, creatures may be created that could already be evolutionarily redundant or were dead ends. Some might be seriously deformed, and thus those experiments would have to be terminated forthwith.

Known as The Invisible Ones, the inhabitants of this new universe would bring a new beginning where the universe started over based on a new turn of the spiral.

Developmentally it would be a step up the ladder to reach a higher dimension. Their universe was intermingled with our own. They did not exist "out there" but were entwined within our own universe, and occupy the same "space" as ours. Indeed, they co-existed and commingled in many other dimensions.

In effect, all eleven dimensions occupied the same space, as if they all intertwined with one another, yet were separate. As an analogy, we see different colors depending on which wavelength of the electromagnetic spectrum we choose to examine. However, all the different colors are a part of the same electromagnetic spectrum.

It is no easy matter creating new universes...

Vran

2. How Life Begins

How did life begin? Before we can shed some light on this topic, some elementary requirements must be fulfilled prior to the creation of life itself. We start from the lowest point when we assert that the universe is multidimensional and that the universe is programmed for life by the Life Force itself.

Lifeforms or organic entities are initially created from the embedded patterns that exist in the higher dimensions. In this way, the patterns of the Life Force already existing in the higher dimensions will be re-used in the lower dimensions, finally to create the lowest or most base dimension that we refer to as the world of three dimensions, with the fourth being referred to as time.

All of the higher dimensions support lifeforms appropriate to the dimension in which they live.

These patterns are themselves created from the laws, patterns, or templates of Reality imprinted on space-time that are centered around a living pattern. This vibrational pattern can be likened to playing music in a different key. The "notes" in each dimension are the same, but played in a different key. The musical notes and the order they are played are the same as before, but are shifted downwards in frequency to create a lower dimension.

An alternative perspective is to describe the entire dimensional complex as forming a living lattice that is almost crystalline in nature.

Life follows this imprint found in the highest dimension (or pattern) of Reality everywhere it manifests, but as local conditions will vary considerably, lifeforms will as a matter of course be significantly different in appearance, function, or form to those found in other parts of the universe—despite having the same foundation.

Life itself must also have an extremely durable platform upon which to develop. The planet(s) or indeed anywhere within space itself where life can take a hold, must be stable over billions of years, uninterrupted by major life extinction events such as collisions with other planetary bodies or even the extinction of its sun.

Evolution will then take hold over the course of that huge expanse of time. The crude creatures that would be initially created will be suited to the conditions in which they are manifested. However, conditions often change drastically over time, so the ability of lifeforms to adapt and evolve is a primary requirement.

It is also the case that while lifeforms may indeed be suited to their current localized conditions, there is a "hidden agenda" that forces all organisms to evolve toward the eventual destiny of a return to the Primal Intelligence.

To show how some aspects of the creation of life may operate, way back in the mists of time scientists conducted experiments that demonstrated that if a test tube of the required raw ingredients was exposed to a magnetic field, which also contained another test tube of already formed DNA, then the exposed raw materials would form themselves into identical DNA.

The first test tube contained only raw chemicals; it was purely the exposure of the base ingredients located in the second test tube to the same enclosing magnetic field that changed the constituents into new DNA.

In other words, exposing one test tube that originally did not contain any DNA to the same magnetic field that already contained an existing test tube of DNA, caused it to form a duplicate.

Somehow, the magnetic field acted as a carrier wave for an energy as yet unquantified that caused the DNA to replicate.

The magnetic waves created or exposed a "pattern" or "blueprint" on which raw ingredients could assemble to form DNA, and therefore duplicate life itself.

It must be stated here that is not within humanity's power to create life from scratch.

3. Fractal Expansion

As an analogy of how the universe might expand from its original point source, imagine an animated fractal image of a flower. The flower grows from its center; each petal that opens forms a duplicate of the last. The petals continue to grow in size as they move towards the periphery, causing the flower to continually increase in size.

The concept is similar to viewing a movie of a fractal but now it runs in reverse. The "flower" does not begin at the periphery with the petals working inwards as conventional fractal images depict, but instead they start forming outwards from its center.

To clarify, the pattern forms from its beginning point (the nucleus), so the patterns (laws of the universe) duplicate themselves ever outwards. They carry the Life Force (as an embedded part of the pattern) into structures of ever-increasing dimensions that are only limited by the constraints of their environments and the laws of Nature that exist in that locality.

It must be stressed here that these so-called laws of the universe are conscious in their own right. We refer to them as demiurges, angels, egregores, and such like. They were brought into Creation to carry out certain functions over the lifetime of the universe.

Reverting now to the previous paragraphs, to recap and amplify, the universe was initially formed from wave patterns that then combined (or devolved) into elemental particles that were themselves formed from the continual expansion of the universal "fractal", which formed into ever-larger conglomerations. As the eleven-dimensional universe expanded, it also brought the patterns of all the elemental waves/particles contained within it.

Thus each wave/particle also incorporated the ability to create life. In other words, life itself was seeded into every atom contained in the entire universe. Therefore in this way, the universe was formed with life already "built in".

This initial, for want of a better phrase, "electromagnetic carrier wave" carried the ingredients for life that originally came from outside this three-dimensional construct from the higher dimensions. In effect, it might be easier to think of the universe as unrolling itself (alternatively: unfolding or unpacking itself), as it expanded into space/time.

As the universe continued to unroll or unpack itself, the additional dimensions also unwrapped or lowered their vibrational frequency (akin to a piano with longer strings producing a lower tone) from the original single eleven-dimensional elemental point to condense into just the three (or four dimensions including time), which are the foundation of the material universe we currently live within.

This fractal universe will at some point reach a maximum size due to the physical laws that constrain it. The universe cannot outgrow the laws that are built into it, so it must inevitably decay, and collapse into black holes or other regressive forms of matter.

The opposite of a black hole is a white hole. These curious beasts expel matter rather than suck it in. As has been pointed out previously in another context, they operate like a fractal in reverse. Matter forms and expands from the inside of the fractal outwards.

When matter has been absorbed due to the suction of the black hole, it is then simultaneously expelled from a white hole. These two events constitute The Reversal during which time stops and then reverses. The cycle repeats almost *ad infinitum* until the Days of Brahma are concluded, and a new intelligence takes over.

The dominant species that is created from this cataclysm will grow to incomprehensible heights of intelligence and understanding during the final epoch. It will have sufficient control over its environment to allow it to proceed unimpeded.

This is the potential turning point where the species itself will determine whether it will survive—or pass into oblivion. It is also at this point that this species will have control of all matter and the patterns or laws embedded within it.

If this unimaginably advanced civilization survives, it creates the conditions for the growth of a new creation out of the cinders of the former universe—like a phoenix rising out of the ashes of the old. They will have themselves become the new Architect.

Life on a Higher Turn of the Spiral

Information

The universe is now on a higher turn of the spiral in the next Day of Brahma.

Although this is a new universe, it occupies the same "space" as that of the older reality. This is because all dimensions are in essence just one. The so-called different dimensions are in actuality a unified framework that is necessary for intelligences to be able to visualize and comprehend the enormity of the scale of the universe and all it contains. In truth then, these dimensional constructs are simply artifacts of the lower realms to aid assimilation.

This oneness makes it possible for higher beings to be able to "read" previous iterations of the universe. In this manner, higher dimensional beings are able to incorporate information from the earlier iterations of previous universes.

The beings known as The Invisible Ones that it contains are no longer solely a part of the three/four-dimensional world. This is now the universe in what we will term the fifth dimension in which different laws operate. Other higher dimensions are yet to fully evolve in a further Day of Brahma, several billion years hence.

To construct this new universe, as always, it is based on ordered principles that in effect form a hierarchy of laws of increasing complexity (or density). These laws or rules must of necessity arise before anything else.

The Invisible Ones are created within the primordial egg, or more colloquially what we shall refer to as the Big Bang; their role being to "unpack" the laws or patterns behind existence.

The dimensions (the patterns situated on top of Reality) will then unfold according to their own laws that are laid down for them. This allows matter to be created (known as a "hot universe"), which is followed by an extended cooling down period that will last for many eons.

As the universe expands, it also unfolds and evolves in the many higher dimensions that cannot be seen or detected by humans, nor their primitive equipment. This is because human beings' senses, or their apparatus, are primarily designed to function within a very limited bandwidth of the electromagnetic spectrum as found within the lesser three dimensions of space plus time.

We may peer into the night sky and visualize an expansion or a contraction of our universe as the dimensions unfold within time over the ages, but even in humanity's own universe, the framework that the universe relies upon resides outside of time in other higher dimensions.

Eventually, civilization will appear if conditions remain stable enough—for long enough. However, many worlds will "die on the vine" before other civilizations that may take millions or even billions of years to develop can flourish. However, perhaps a few will survive, such as The Invisible Ones who exist in a living crystal city.

As a matter of fact, their "beingness" comprises the city itself, because everything is created from vibrations. The buildings and other structures are the beings themselves—or rather they are the city's frequencies that resemble living crystals in structure.

As an example, interacting sound frequencies create "nodes", or more clearly, under certain conditions the frequencies beat together, rather like old-fashioned airplane engines that are not quite in synchrony.

The buildings and other structures are the beings themselves—or rather, they are composed of frequencies that resemble living crystals in form.

Matter in their world is created from the use of vibrations (as we currently understand them) in the form of the electromagnetic spectrum. For example, in the case of the wavelength of light, when photons are passed though the double slit experiment, light may show itself as a wave, but then again under different conditions it can be viewed as particulate in nature.

To communicate the "residents" alter their crystals' pitch. For example, sometimes the note would be higher in pitch, sometimes lower, but never non-existent, as that would entail instant non-existence or death.

To those more technically inclined, these beings alter their frequency so that they are in synchrony. One party will then alter its frequency slightly to create a "beat frequency" in a similar fashion to listening to binaural beat tones or music through headphones.

To create binaural beats, each headphone will play a slightly different tone to the headphone on the other ear, and thus the brain in the middle will "hear" a third sympathetic tone, different in frequency to either of the original tones. This is similar in concept to the old FM (Frequency Modulation) radios used back on ancient Terra.

These beings are also able to change color by using slight variations in frequency. For example, red is a "lower" form of vibration and can denote a hot-tempered person, or one who exhibits rage. At the other end of the spectrum, the color blue/violet is reserved for the "higher" functions of the mind.

The Invisible Ones also use a concept similar to orbital resonance in which one planet will orbit in synchrony with another. To enlarge on this concept, one planet may revolve around its sun three times, to four or more revolutions of its neighbor. In other words, the planets will have different "frequencies" but always keep in step with one another.

To illustrate: In the Sol solar system, Jupiter's moons Io, Europa, and Ganymede exist in a stable resonance with each other; while at the same time the asteroid Griqua is in a 2:1 resonance with Jupiter while simultaneously the asteroid Alinda is in a 3:1 resonance with it.

Resonance in celestial mechanics is known to operate everywhere in the known universe. For example, four of the planets of the nearby star Kepler-223 (a star in the vicinity of Sol) are also confirmed to be in resonance.

Another planetary system, about 100 light years from Sol (HD 110067), has six known planets in resonant orbits. The innermost planet orbits three times for every two orbits of the next outermost planet. Similarly, the same 3:2 resonance also holds for the second and third planets as well as the third and fourth planets.

The fourth planet also orbits four times for every three times for the fifth planet out in a 4:3 resonance. Additionally, the last but one (the fifth planet), orbits with the sixth planet out in this same 4:3 resonance.

In addition, the innermost planet completes six orbits in exactly the same period as the outermost (sixth) of the planets completes just one orbit.

The mind-boggling thing is that each planet has kept its neighbor in check in this steady rhythm for billions of years, thus possibly creating many of the right conditions for intelligent life to evolve.

Vran

1. The Crystal City

As stated, much of The Invisible Ones' world was created solely by the action of mental activity. To create something, it was only necessary to bring the desired object to consciousness, and then focus on the concept "Be!" and it will be so.

The only proviso was to recall that all things are One. This concept was based around quantum entanglement, or as one scientist long ago named Einstein referred to it, "spooky action at a distance". Right up until his death, despite his genius, Einstein couldn't grasp the staggering implications of the, at the time, new quantum mechanics.

Travel was also found to be an operation of the mind. In the era of this distant epoch of which we now speak, physical travel had long since faded away. It was only necessary to mentally focus on the coordinates of the desired location, and it was done. It was more of a shift of consciousness rather than physically moving from one location to another.

Communication between one member of this species and another was also an interesting concept. While all is one via quantum entanglement, if a certain part of the whole could be isolated into the form of just a single entity, then if it wanted to communicate with another part, that being would then alter its whole frequency slightly. As an analogy, imagine Jell-O (a jelly) that had just been released from its mold after being taken from the fridge. It wobbled and shook, but still stayed whole. Similarly, the other part of the singularity felt the vibration and responded in kind.

These beings were of a different form altogether than anything that had gone before, yet something still remained of their human attributes. They were still fully human in consciousness, despite bearing little physical resemblance to their forebears. Their humanness stemmed from their "beingness" that resided in their heart center.

The heart is not just a mechanical pump, but is at the very core of what it is to be human. The operation of the heart is still a mystery, but it is said that its origin belongs in another dimension.

We must now contemplate the concept of these beings who live entirely within these higher dimensions. To those of us who exist solely within the conventional three/four-dimensional world (3+1), they would at best appear to be invisible, but their presence could possibly be traceable by registering their actions.

In essence, The Invisible Ones could only reveal themselves in the lower four dimensions by using the false worlds of images and forms that are then assembled within the human mind, but do not represent the true external world that is sometimes referred to as Reality.

At best, The Invisible Ones could only project their images and thoughts in a distorted guise, which to use an analogy, may resemble the distorted images found in fairground mirrors that twist and turn everything out of shape.

Nevertheless, The Invisible Ones who existed (and who still exist) in the fifth (or higher) dimensions could still view objects in the lower dimensions, just as we are able to see two-dimensional structures or forms while still remaining situated in a three-dimensional universe. However, those in some of the higher dimensions (in a similar manner to ourselves) cannot see into the higher realities that are "above their pay grade".

The Invisible Ones herald a new beginning where the universe began again based on a new turn of the spiral. Evolutionarily it was a further step up the ladder that would continue to advance into other even higher dimensions in the future Days of Brahma.

While they are as unaware (as we ourselves are) of what the future may hold, there are specially trained individuals who could traverse space and time. Known as The Travelers, they had been selected at birth for their special abilities. They used certain specialized equipment to amplify their sensitivities. For example, they utilized a type of Kozyrev mirror in which The Traveler could foresee probabilities in the future, along with those existent in the past.

It must be borne in mind that their conception of time was entirely different to that found in our own understanding. Intelligences existing in each of the higher dimensions will have different "versions" or understandings of the nature of space and time in which different "rules" or "patterns" would apply.

All versions of reality are valid, but depend on the dimensional sphere and vibrational rate in which they live. As in the story of the elephant in the dark, what the scholars understand of true Reality depends on which part they have got a hold of.

2. Foracks

Foracks the hermaphrodite steadied himself/herself/itself as he entered a vertical highly polished metallic chamber similar in concept to a type of Kozyrev mirror that had been designed and constructed to focus his Life Force.

He had been trained for many eons for this task, his all-consuming mission. His mission was to initiate the beginning of life itself.

Foracks had travelled a very, very long way from home. Though this place occupied the same "location" as the older versions of the universe, dimensionally it was eons away from previous forms. Here he was limited to just three plus one dimensions that were comprised of mostly rigid forms, patterns and laws.

It wasn't until it was discovered that the universe (more correctly referred to as Reality) had neither beginning nor end that those beings whose natural home was in the three plus one dimensions, let alone those entities from some of the higher dimensions, could understand that the Life Force itself could not be created.

Further progress could only be entertained once it was understood that the Life Force may only be transported from one time to another, or from one location to a different locale. Simply put, it could only be initiated, and not manufactured or created.

However, The Invisible Ones, who were not composed of matter as we understand it, had to wait for much time to pass before conditions allowed the possibility of creating a device that was capable of dimensional time travel. Not only was it necessary to accomplish the already incredible feat of voyaging within time, but also to be able to travel down through the dimensions on the same occasion.

In this formless epoch, it was not possible to single out one particular period of time from the whole gamut of others or— more explicitly—pick one era of time from a continuum in which everything appeared to overlap, or be fused together. In essence then, developmentally this epoch was seemingly a totally featureless landscape. It was not until higher intelligences arose, that it became possible to differentiate one era from another.

Thus in those very early times there initially seemed to be no substantial differences. As we have just mentioned, an epoch that comprised a small part of the continuum would thus appear to the casual eye to be much the same as any other.

However, once sentient life had gained a foothold, evolution would occur at an ever-increasing pace similar in graph form to a bell-curve, and see to it that intelligent beings eventually arose who were advanced enough to function as pilots or navigators for such dimensionless and featureless forms of travel.

Described as the Days of Brahma, in essence the evolution of the universe was the slow painful progression of humanity toward its eventual destiny as the overseer of Creation itself.

It was impossible for Foracks to visit such a huge number of worlds to seed the Life Force, thus one aspect of his/her/its function was to create and deploy minuscule metallic spheres not much larger than the diameter of a hair, which contained the vitality of life complete with preserving compounds able to withstand the sometimes huge expanses of time. Foracks would then release them into the void of space to find their own way. Eventually they might land on some far-off world that hosted the right conditions for life to take a foothold and then evolve into higher lifeforms.

Essentially, these tiny spheres or spores were spewed out by a huge cigar-shaped electromagnetic craft, several miles in length, that travelled broadside in orbit around the planet. Its north and south poles were aligned with the electromagnetic field of the world around which it was orbiting to create a circular ring formation that surrounded the planet. These rings eventually dissipated over time into space by the action of the centrifugal forces created by the machines.

The core notion was to allow these seeds that contained the germ of life and thus the spark of consciousness to grow into forms that would most likely be fundamentally different in format or function to that found on any other world. However, the seeds would all still contain the beginnings of life that helped to construct an intricate web that contained all beings—no matter which their native star system or planet may eventually end up as their home.

For instance, Foracks' spores may, in the deep reaches of time, settle in the far-off Andromeda galaxy. The Life Force dispersed there might flourish and evolve for many eons before gaining the means for their future evolutionary offspring to travel the depths of space to seek out other beings similar to themselves, who perhaps in like manner would also have been created to further the task of the propagation and dissemination of the singular Life Force.

Foracks understood that his own task would take many millennia to complete in this three-dimensional universe that is bound by its own unique laws of material existence. He knew too, that since entering this world of mortality, he must endure within the constraints of space and time in order to carry out his designated task.

His natural freedom that originally came from a world where the laws of nature were entirely different to those found here were for the present temporarily suspended.

He earnestly hoped that his willing sacrifice would be understood in the far reaches of time. While he did not crave recognition or reward, he wished that others who would follow him would emulate his lead as best they could.

Foracks settled himself in the chamber and waited while the patterns of the universe were adjusted into a suitable configuration that would allow him to travel into the distant past.

Initially, only his consciousness could make the journey, but as planetary conditions improved, his corporeal body would be fabricated from the crude materials available in the new environment that surrounded him.

To aid in understanding his undertaking, life was initially infused from lifeless materials that eventually evolved into simple cellular organisms, which further developed into multicellular creatures that were able to evolve even further.

Eventually, Foracks' distant descendants might develop a consciousness able to comprehend his task, and then eventually evolve into the beings that are united with the Life Force itself in a symbiotic relationship beneficial to all.

After some time, Foracks opened the door of his capsule to a world totally devoid of life. He discovered a foreboding red sky, scorching steaming rocks, rivers of bubbling white-hot lava, and clouds of noxious gasses. If he had been fully materialized in this foreboding place, he would have died instantly from exposure to the heat, and the many hazardous chemicals that would have soon choked him to death.

He thought wryly, "What is this hostile environment that I have now arrived in?" A thought flashed into his mind just before he dismissed it as he recalled his task, "Undoubtedly it appears that The Overseers have been sadly mistaken in sending me to this barren inhospitable hellhole of a planet."

Then he quickly recalled that what he saw here were just the primordial beginnings of a world that one day would harbor sweet fragrant air, oxygen-giving trees, white puffy clouds in an azure blue sky, chirping birds on the wing, and human beings themselves.

Regretfully he realized that he would never see those halcyon days, though his actions and his essence would be contained in the very Life Force itself that all beings throughout Eternity would share. His duty was to sacrifice himself on behalf of The Overseers for this, his most monumental of deeds.

He kept these images of this world yet to come in his thoughts as he set about his designated tasks. First, he must create the organic conditions for life, and then he must utilize the machinery that would spread the Life Force to other worlds that may themselves eventually harbor life—as this planet would also shortly accomplish. He must then set that same "machinery" in motion to terraform this world so that eventually it would become hospitable to higher lifeforms.

Most of this so-called "machinery" was in fact situated in other dimensions and could not be considered mechanical or electrical in nature at all. Instead, the machinery was designed to manipulate the patterns or laws of space/time to obtain the desired effect.

However, much of this machinery must necessarily protrude into the lower material dimensions in order to fulfil its function here. The machines in the lower dimensions were then designed to manipulate forms of energies and plasma in the process of creating usable forms that were both organic and inorganic in composition.

Foracks bent to peer at his instruments once again. He muttered to himself in satisfaction, "Hmm, the encapsulation process of The Life Force is now complete. The Life Force and the necessary compounds and nutrients to sustain it have now been inserted into tiny metallic spheroids that are small enough to float lazily down through the atmosphere of myriad alien worlds without harm."

He knew that the tiny spheroids would, in a similar fashion to spiders living far in the future, float down almost weightlessly on the breeze, and so would be able to withstand what would otherwise surely have been a fiery entry into an atmosphere that would destroy the fragile Life Force encased within.

Embedded in each minuscule orb was a small quantity of materials that supported and protected the fragile Life Force. The tiny spheres would then—possibly in the many millennia to come—land upon new worlds that would become the Life Force's new home, even as far as many of the most distant galaxies.

Satisfied, Foracks pressed a button on his screen that would release the enormous clouds of billions upon billions of these minute capsules from the gigantic electromagnetic plasma gun situated high in orbit above this world. Trillions of these tiny metallic spheres containing the Life Force would be released almost *ad infinitum*, each ready to seek out its new home.

As far as Foracks' current situation could now be explained, his physical form had now been devised and situated on a world that had not long ago (in geological terms) been created from seeming chaos.

This element of his work to disperse the capsules was now complete. Now it was the turn of this inhospitable world on which he now stood to be terraformed, accompanied by a similar action on myriad other planets.

Foracks decided at this point to give this hellish planet a name so that it would have a singular identity. In essence in another universe and dimension, this time and place would have become the planet Terra.

He decided to call this world Ki. The label arose from the name given to the circulating life energy within a living being. Having a name would also help to solidify its identity and thus its purpose. Having its own uniqueness would assist him in focusing his mind on the remaining tasks ahead.

He visualized the beings this planet would eventually host as bearing the name *Homo Sapiens Sapiens*. But this dream was from far, far away in the distant future and belonged to a different dimension. Evolution had a very long way to go before it could ever possibly create such beings.

His body still partly residing in a higher dimension, Foracks stepped out onto the still hot ground to search for items that he could use to terraform this place. But there were none. So he used the vitality of Life itself in the form of primitive anaerobic bacteria that he had brought with him. Foracks and these primitive organisms could live without oxygen. Both were necessary for this stage of his task. For many millennia these primitive bacteria would work tirelessly to harness this raw world before their task was done.

Many millennia later, Foracks initiated The Great Oxygenation Event. It was necessary for these simple anaerobic lifeforms to eventually die so that more advanced multicellular lifeforms that were able to breathe oxygen could develop and evolve. The primitive non-oxygen-breathing organisms had initially provided the right conditions for the newer aerobic lifeforms to flourish. Essentially these early bacteria had sacrificed themselves by working toward their own extinction.

Foracks' lifespan was long, but not infinite. He had been able to kick-start evolution on its long rocky road before he was to die when his work was completed. His assignment was now almost finished, and it was now the task of his fellow higher beings to take the reins and oversee this still fragile world and its contents.

He opened the airlock to his chamber, and stepped outside and took a deep breath. The aerobic atmosphere was poisonous to him, so he died where he stood. His lifeless body was cast aside on this now fertile planet.

The Overseers mourned their loss, but could only look on from their higher-dimensional world as his body quickly deteriorated from the actions of furious dust storms that sandpapered the flesh from his white bones. The ravages of time had exacted their toll. But his body was not his essence. His essential being was welcomed back to its real home amongst The Overseers, who greeted his life spirit with open arms.

Situated outside of the space/time continuum as we know it, The Overseers had waited long eons for evolution to catch up. Much time passed before Ki, which would eventually become Terra, was able to fulfill its duty and embody consciousness in beings capable of manipulating their environment. Many more long millennia also passed before these creatures were sufficiently endowed with intelligence, and thus could be granted the responsibility of self-determination to become stewards of their world, and beyond.

There were many false starts. These primitive hominid creatures on many occasions not only nearly destroyed themselves, but at the same time compromised their entire ecosystem. It was during these times that The Overseers steered events, often by using subtle "prods" in the right direction that evolution often required to avert disaster and stay on track.

Foracks had not died in vain. His DNA (or pattern) was imprinted in the very fabric or design of the universe. In time, many eons hence, his DNA would be recovered to form the basis of his distant familial analog Aiden.

Foracks' "pattern", which was now embedded in the universe, would successively evolve to become Aiden, who himself had been tasked with transforming the universe into its next iteration. One might remark here that there was a long bloodline of evolved beings whose task was to guide the fledgling human race along its evolutionary path.

While this could not exactly be termed reincarnation, this concept may be thought of as a major evolutionary progression using the patterns embedded in the matrix of space/time as its model.

To accomplish this task, it would need the next universe to be born and born yet again, almost *ad infinitum*, to be guided and molded by their exemplars in higher dimensions. However, the human race still had a very long way to go before it could be tasked with the role of vicegerent.

Only a fool worked without a backup and The Highest Impulse was no exception. Foracks understood this, so even if his own project failed, the six planets around the distant star HD 110067 had already been primed for intelligent life, and were ready and waiting.

Their orbits would be stable for billions of years—just long enough for intelligences on a parallel track to humanity to form and come to fruition…

Time

Is in the eye of the beholder.

The past belongs to the future,

And the future belongs to the past.

All is One.

The spiral of life goes round and round,

Painfully creeping ever upwards,

For evermore…

Ella

Influences in Formulating This Book

There are way too many to mention here, but the works of Arthur C. Clarke, H.G. Wells, Isaac Asimov and many more of the classical science fiction writers influenced me most in the world of sci-fi, while many others have also impressed me greatly. Here are just a few books, movies, etc. that were formative in bringing this volume to fruition:

Science Fiction:

Dune	Frank Herbert
Childhood's End	Arthur C. Clarke
2001: A Space Odyssey (movie)	Arthur C. Clarke
2010: Odyssey Two (movie)	Arthur C. Clarke
The City and the Stars	Arthur C. Clarke
Foundation	Isaac Asimov
Foundation and Empire	Isaac Asimov
Second Foundation	Isaac Asimov
Canopus in Argos: Archives	Doris Lessing

Other topics include:

The numerous works of	Idries Shah
The People of the Secret	Ernest Scott

Godhead – The Brain's Big Bang	J. Griffin, I. Tyrrell
All and Everything	G.I. Gurdjieff
The Theory of Celestial Influence	Rodney Collin
Lucky Planet	David Waltham
Hyperspace	Michio Kaku
The Grand Biocentric Design: How Life Creates Reality	
	Robert Lanza *et al.*
A Journey through Cosmic Consciousness	Wez Jamroz
CosMos	Ervin Laszlo *et al.*

Websites of interest include:

NASA:

http://www.nasa.gov/

Idries Shah Foundation:

http://www.idriesshahfoundation.org/

The Tradition in the West:

https://web.archive.org/web/20200123010301/http://www.real
sufism.com/

The Oscillating Universe:

http://www.theoscillatinguniverse.co.uk/

Electric Universe:

http://www.electricuniverse.info/Introduction

Lucidity Institute:

http://www.lucidity.com/index.html

Institute of HeartMath:

http://www.heartmath.org/

Human Givens Institute:

http://www.hgi.org.uk/archive/human-givens.htm

Masaru Emoto:

http://www.masaru-emoto.net/english/index.html

Kardashev scale:

Wikipedia: https://en.wikipedia.org/wiki/Kardashev_scale

And: https://veronicasicoe.com/2014/04/12/the-kardashev-scale-0-to-6/

Breath of Brahma:

https://www.bibliotecapleyades.net/universo/cosmos398.htm

Electron-Hole combination:

https://en.wikipedia.org/wiki/Light-emitting_diode

And: https://en.wikipedia.org/wiki/Electron_hole

Note: As far as is practical, all future calendar days and dates given in this book were calculated and checked for accuracy at:

https://web.archive.org/web/20120716225219/http://www.ortelius.de/kalender/form_en2.php

About the Author

Julian Hadlow is an author and spiritual traveler. He has spent approximately thirty years studying religion, philosophy, communication, and psychology. He brings to his writing his experience, wisdom, insights, and an eagerness to help others.

As part of his quest, he spearheaded the What We Have in Common Project (https://whatwehaveincommon.org/), profiling insights into human nature.

Should you be interested in ordering additional copies of this book, it is available on Amazon.com and elsewhere.

For more information, please visit his website or Facebook page.

Go to:

www.xerseschronicles.com

Or:

www.facebook.com/xerseschronicles

Now you have completed this book—did you enjoy it?

Reviews are the lifeblood of an author.

If you "got it" then I invite you to review the book on Amazon, and/or Goodreads.com.

Thank you!

www.ingramcontent.com/pod-product-compliance
Lightning Source LLC
Chambersburg PA
CBHW060916180626
46817CB00004B/1276